INVE

THE RESTAURANT
OF LOVE REGAINED

THE RESTAURANT OF LOVE REGAINED

ITO OGAWA

Translated by
David Karashima

ALMA BOOKS

ALMA BOOKS LTD
London House
243–253 Lower Mortlake Road
Richmond
Surrey TW9 2LL
United Kingdom
www.almabooks.com

Shokudô Katatsumuri
Copyright © Ito Ogawa, 2008
First published in Japan in 2008 by Poplar Publishing Co., Ltd
English language translation rights arranged with Poplar Publishing Co., Ltd
through Japan Foreign-Rights Centre
The Restaurant of Love Regained first published by Alma Books Limited in 2011
English translation © David Karashima, 2011

Ito Ogawa asserts her moral right to be identified as the author of this work
in accordance with the Copyright, Designs and Patents Act 1988

Printed in Great Britain by CPI Mackays

ISBN: 978-1-84688-149-7

THE RESTAURANT
OF LOVE REGAINED

I CAME HOME FROM my part-time job at the Turkish restaurant to find my apartment empty. Literally everything was gone. The television, the washer, the fridge, the lights, the curtains. Even the entrance mat had been taken! Not a single thing had been spared. For a moment, I wanted to believe I'd walked into the wrong apartment. But no matter how many times I checked, there was no changing the fact I was standing in the love nest I'd shared with my Indian boyfriend, with its heart-shaped stain on the ceiling staring down as indelible evidence.

The entire place looked exactly as it had when the estate agent had first showed it to me. In fact, the only thing different was the slight scent of garam masala that hung in the air and the key I'd had cut for my boyfriend, which now sat catching the light in the middle of the bare living-room floor. Each night, my boyfriend and I had slept here, holding hands under the covers of the futon in this apartment I'd gone through so much trouble to rent. His skin had always carried a scent of exotic spices, and there were photo postcards of the river Ganges taped along the window sill. I could never read the ornate Hindi script on those cards, but whenever I touched them it felt like holding hands with his family in India. I wondered if I'd be going there with him some day. And what an Indian wedding would be like. My daydreams were as sweet as mango lassi.

The room had been crammed full of keepsakes that we'd accumulated in the three years we'd been living there, with each evoking a precious memory of our time spent together. Every night, I'd cook in our small kitchen as I waited for him to return for dinner. It was a smallish kitchen with a small kitchen sink. But I liked the tiling that went all around it. It was a corner apartment, so there were windows along three walls to let in plenty of light. Some of the happiest moments in my life were when I'd come home from an early shift and basked in the orange sun that streamed in from the western sky while cooking dinner.

We even had a simple gas oven. There was also a little window by the kitchen, so the smells never lingered whenever I cooked dried fish for myself. This kitchen had been the home to my beloved kitchen utensils too. There was the hundred-year-old pestle and mortar that belonged to my late grandmother, a container made of Japanese cypress that I'd used for keeping rice, a Le Creuset enamel pot I'd bought with my first pay cheque, a set of long-serving chopsticks with extra fine tips I'd found in a speciality shop in Kyoto, an Italian paring knife given to me on my twentieth birthday by the owner of an organic-vegetables shop, a comfortable cotton apron, jade gravel I used for making pickled aubergine, and the traditional cast-iron *nambu* frying pan I'd travelled as far north as Morioka to buy. It was a collection of quality items built to last a lifetime. A collection accumulated over an eternity with whatever I could spare from my meagre monthly pay cheque. And now it was gone.

In a moment of misplaced hope, I opened and searched each and every one of the kitchen cabinets, but my fingers grasped at nothing but air that seemed to hold a hint of what had once been there – the jar of plums my grandmother and I had pickled together, carefully wiping down each one as we went, and the couscous and other ingredients I'd gathered for the cream croquette for my vegetarian boyfriend that evening.

Suddenly, a thought dawned on me and I ran out of the door in my socks. I'd remembered the only Japanese fermented food my boyfriend had been partial to – the vegetables we'd pickled in salted rice-bran paste. It was something he ate every day without exception, and only the bran paste from my grandmother could give it that special flavour he liked. I'd kept its vase in a small closet by the front door, where the temperature and humidity were always just right – being cooler than the rest of the apartment through the summer but warmer than the fridge in winter. Delicious and homely, it was a keepsake evocative of precious moments with my grandmother and I prayed for it still to be there.

As I opened the door and peered inside, I was delighted to find it was there, sitting silently, waiting for me in the dark. I opened its lid and checked inside, relieved to find it just as I'd left it after smoothing its surface with my hand that morning, with the tips of several light-green leaves poking through. I thought of how each of these leaves led to a stalk that was in turn attached to an aubergine, peeled and with an "X" carved into its side, helping it to soak up the sweet juices and wonderful flavours. Overjoyed that the vase was safe, I swept it up in my arms and cradled it to my chest, feeling its cool ceramic surface against my body – my only remaining worldly possession.

After replacing the lid of the heavy vase, I struggled to tuck it under one arm. Then I returned to the main room, scooped the key up off the floor with my toes, held my basket in my other hand and walked out of my desolate apartment, letting the door slam shut loudly behind me as if closing a chapter of my life. Then, instead of taking the lift, I chose to take the stairs, moving carefully so as not to trip and drop the vase, and set off on my way.

Outside, the moon floated full in the eastern sky and I turned back for another glance at my thirty-year-old building, standing still in the darkness like some over-sized monster. I remembered when I'd first found the place and how I'd convinced the landlord to let us rent the apartment, despite us having no guarantor, by sending him a batch of my fresh home-baked madeleines. Then we'd moved in and made it our own. *Our* love nest. And there was no way I could bear to stay there if I was to be alone.

I stopped off at my landlord's place to return the key. It was the end of the month and I'd already paid the next month's rent. The contract had clearly stated that tenants were required to give a full month's notice when leaving. But since I had paid up already and all the furniture was already gone, I figured there should be no problem about me leaving right away.

Since I didn't have a watch or a mobile phone, I couldn't tell what time it was. But I knew where I needed to go. So I dragged my feet through the dark streets, walking the equivalent of several stops along the train line until I came to the main bus terminal. Then I spent most of what money I had left on getting myself a ticket for the overnight bus – the one that would take me back to the village I'd left at the age of fifteen but had never returned to since.

Almost as soon as I boarded with my rice-bran vase in my arms, the bus started up and took off. I sat by the window and watched the city lights pass me by. "Goodbye," I thought, giving the city a wave in my mind. Then I closed my eyes and let the stressful events of the day disperse like leaves in the autumn wind.

My mother's house was in a quiet village surrounded by mountains. Nature was all around and I loved that place from the bottom of my heart. But on the night of my high-school graduation, I'd boarded a night bus – like the one I was on now – and set off on a one-way journey. Since that day, my only contact with my mother had been through the exchange of New Year's cards. Several years after I left home, my mother sent me a New Year's card bearing a photo of her dressed as a street performer, sitting shoulder to shoulder with her new pet in a flowery dress. That's how I found out that my mum had replaced me with a pet pig.

When I'd first arrived in the city as a fifteen-year-old, I'd stayed at my grandmother's place. And ever since then, whenever I'd returned, I'd call out, "I'm home!" as I rattled those old sliding doors open to see her standing in the doorway of the kitchen, welcoming me with the warmest of smiles. Grandmother was my mother's mother. She lived in an old house on the outskirts of the city and her lifestyle was far from luxurious. But she knew how to make the most of the simple pleasures in life, treasuring each passing day and moving in harmony with the changing seasons. She spoke with elegance and had a soft demeanour. But beneath that she was strong and self-confident. She was also one of those women who looked great in a kimono. I loved her. I loved being with her. And the ten years since I first arrived at her place had passed in the blink of an eye.

I wiped the mist off the window and stared beyond my reflection, watching the skyscrapers grow smaller behind us and the highway that snaked along in front. Except for occasionally trimming my fringe, I hadn't really cut my hair since I'd met my boyfriend. I'd left it long because he liked it that way and I'd parted it down the middle with a braid on each side that hung down to the middle of my back. I stared at my face in the window again and opened my mouth wide, swallowing down the sodium-yellow-and-black scenery beyond like a humpback whale breathing in a ton of krill. And at that moment, for just a split second, I locked eyes with myself from the past. I thought I'd caught a glimpse of myself ten years ago, sitting on a bus on the other side of the highway, headed in the other direction – my nose pressed up against the window, my mind buzzing with big-city lights. Immediately, I glanced back at the bus as it passed on by. But the moment was gone. With one bus headed towards the past and the other towards the future, the gap between us grew quickly until it disappeared altogether in the mist that clung to the window.

I don't know precisely when, but at some point I'd decided I wanted to be a professional chef. But my culinary career had been like a transient rainbow in the fading evening light. I'd worked hard in the big city until I'd learnt to talk and to laugh just like the rest of them. Then, one day, my grandmother drew her last quiet breath. I remember coming home late from my job at the Turkish restaurant and finding her. She looked as if she was sleeping next to the low table in the living room, with a delicate napkin covering a plate of doughnuts in the middle. I held my ear to her flat chest, but there was no beat to be heard. I held my hand close to her mouth and nose, but there was no breath to be felt. She was gone and I knew that, so there was no need to call for help. So instead I decided to spend one last night with her. Just her and I, together.

I sat by her side and ate doughnuts all night long as her lifeless body became cold and stiff. I'll never forget the heartwarming taste of those doughnuts – lightly fried in sesame oil, with a delicate sprinkling of poppy seeds and just a dusting of cinnamon and brown sugar. Memories of my grandmother surfaced like bubbles with every bite. Memories of days bathed in warm sunlight. Of my grandmother's pale, veined hand turning the bran in her vase. Her small, rounded back working hard. Her profile as she placed a small taster of her cooking in her hand and carried it to her mouth. The memories kept on coming, floating in and out of my consciousness.

It had been during this difficult time that I'd met my boyfriend. From Monday to Friday, he worked as a waiter at the Indian restaurant next door to my Turkish restaurant. On the weekends he was a musician in their belly-dancing show. We first ran into each other when we were taking the rubbish out back. And from there we'd progressed to chatting during our breaks and on the way home after work. He was tall, kind, and had beautiful eyes. He was a little younger than me and could only speak a little Japanese. But his awkward language skills combined with his smile helped me forget, even if only for a second now and then, the devastating void left by my grandmother's passing.

When I think back on that time, beautiful images of India and Turkey overlap in my mind. For some reason, I always picture a majestic mosque and a beautiful blue sea stretching out behind my boyfriend, as he sits eating beans and vegetable curry, looking every inch the quintessential Indian with his dark skin and clear eyes. This overlapping of images in my mind no doubt came from the restaurants we'd worked in when we met. By that time, I'd been working at the Turkish restaurant for just under five years, which was the longest I'd ever worked anywhere. I was only a part-time employee, but I worked just as many hours as a full-timer. And for the second half of my five-year stint, I'd been working in the kitchen, helping the chefs from Turkey make authentic dishes.

People constantly came and went during my time at the restaurant and I soon became overwhelmed by the constant waves of goodbyes and nice-to-meet-yous. The trick was to take a short-term view and live each day at a time. But when I look back on those days now, I realize those days were special. Miraculous, even.

Realizing I should probably call the Turkish restaurant, I let out a sigh. Then I stared at the reflection in the window, with drops of condensation framing a view of passengers sleeping peacefully in their seats and a stretch of transparent blue darkness beyond that heralded the end of the night.

I opened the window to get some fresh air and stretched my back. The sky was slowly turning white and there was a faint smell of salt in the air. I could see rows of white wind turbines standing tall in the grasslands and turning at speed. I also felt cold, with my knee-length skirt, high socks and long T-shirt doing little to stop the chill that seemed to seep in through every pore of my skin. Even the tips of my nails seemed to be feeling the cold.

When the doors hissed open at my destination, the scent of rain drifted in from far away and I stepped out onto the roundabout of a sad-looking station. The place had changed so little, it was almost as if I'd only been gone for a day. Only, the colours had faded, leaving the whole place drained and washed out, as if someone had sketched the whole scene with pastels, then tried half-heartedly to rub it away.

I had more than an hour to kill before my connecting minibus arrived. So I walked into a nearby convenience store, with its freshly waxed floor exuding the only sense of newness around, and bought some flip cards and a black marker pen with whatever pocket change I could find. Unwrapping the flip cards, I sat down and began to write out the words I'd be needing to use on a daily basis – one word per card to make them as easy to use as possible.

Hello.

Good morning.

The weather is beautiful.

How are you?

Could I have this?

Thank you very much.

Nice to meet you.

Bye. Have a nice day.

Please.

Excuse me. Sorry.

Go ahead.

How much is this?

13

I did this because I had realized something. Could it have been when I was buying the bus ticket? Or when I'd gone to return my key to the landlord? No, it was before that. It was when I'd walked into my room to find it empty. I had lost my voice.

I guess it must have been a physical reaction to the mental shock I'd suffered. But it wasn't the case that my voice had just become hoarse. It was more than that. I simply wasn't able to talk. As if my voice had been completely switched off. Like when someone turns the volume of the radio all the way down. So the music, the voice, the melodies were all there. They just couldn't be heard by anyone.

I was surprised at this discovery. But there was no pain; no discomfort. It didn't hurt and it didn't itch. If anything, it somehow made me feel a little lighter. I'd even been thinking on the bus about how I never wanted to talk to anyone ever again. So I guess it had worked out perfectly. All I could do was focus on my inner voice, the only voice I could hear. I knew this somehow made sense. But I also knew, from my twenty-five years of life experience, that I wouldn't be able to go far without interacting with others.

I took out my flip cards and wrote on the last one "I have temporarily lost my voice". Then I climbed aboard the cheap minibus. Unlike the other bus that had raced through the night, the minibus ambled along at a much slower pace. In time, the sun came over the horizon and my stomach started to rumble. Then I remembered my rice ball left over from yesterday's lunch and took it out of my basket, leaving behind a handkerchief, some tissue paper and a wallet containing just a handful of loose change.

I'd made rice balls every morning to take to work. The Turkish restaurant where I worked was too cheap to provide free meals for its staff and my boyfriend and I were doing our best to save money so that one day we could open up a restaurant of our own. For a moment, I wondered if there was any chance this plan might still go ahead. Then those thoughts were washed away, as if a bucket of white paint had been poured right through my mind.

I'd kept all the money we'd been saving in a closet instead of a bank. There were ten-thousand-yen notes in one-hundred-thousand-yen piles. And whenever we'd accumulated ten piles – or a million yen – I'd put them in a sealed envelope and hid them in a rolled-up futon we no longer used. I wondered how many envelopes there'd been in the end. There was more than one. That much was for sure. But before I could think just how much we'd managed to save, down came another bucket of paint to mask my tarnished dreams.

Unwrapping the wrinkled aluminium foil, I took out the half-crushed rice ball, popped it into my hand and carried it to my mouth. At its heart was the last piece of plum I'd ever pickled with my grandmother and for some reason it tasted unfamiliar. We'd taken turns checking on the pickled plums at night to make sure they didn't develop mould. Then we'd put them out to dry in the summer, laying them out on the veranda for three whole days, during which time we'd massage them with our fingers every three hours or so to soften up the fibres within. Gradually, my grandmother's pickled plums turned a beautiful shade of pink. She didn't even have to add a sprig of red perilla to lend them colour.

I sat there, frozen, for a while, with the last morsel of pickled plum in my mouth. Its sour heart reaching into the very core of my being, its taste more valuable to me than any hidden treasure. As my heart filled up with memories of days spent with my grandmother, tears threatened to overflow from my eyes and spill down my cheeks. But somehow, I managed to keep my despair in a knot that sat somewhere around my throat.

It had been my grandmother who had first taken my hand and led me gently into the world of cookery. At first, I'd just watched. But soon enough, I was standing alongside her in the kitchen, absorbing her many culinary secrets. This was how I'd learnt. Not from my grandmother using words. But from her giving me a tasting at every step of the way. Through this physical experience, I learnt to recognize how different textures worked together and how much salt was just right for each kind of dish.

Things were different at my mother's house, where cooking consisted of little more than popping open cans or heating things in the microwave. But my grandmother made absolutely everything herself – her own miso, her own soy sauce, even her own sun-dried radishes. I remember being absolutely astonished when I first learnt just how much effort goes into making a single bowl of proper miso soup, with its dried sardines, bonito, soy beans and fermented rice. And those are just the basic ingredients! When she was cooking up her magic, it was as if my grandmother was enveloped in a glorious aura. And when I stood by her side, I felt I was a part of something sacred.

At first, the words my grandmother used to describe differing amounts of seasoning such as *tekitou* and *anbai* were like another language to me. But I gradually came to understand what they meant. They were soft terms with rounded edges that painted a vague picture of the appropriate amount of flavour, and only those words could describe the resultant state of perfection.

In my mouth, the pickled plum had all but melted away, leaving only a tiny seed on my tongue with the fading memories of my grandmother. I glanced out of the window. Autumn had already arrived in the village, but there were traces of summer still lingering. After finishing my

17

rice ball, I felt a slight chill run through me and I wished I had a hot drink. But I was already perched on the back seat of the bus, with nowhere to get something to drink and no money in my pocket to pay for one. So instead, I cradled the bran vase on my lap, hoping it would somehow help to keep me warm. Then I pressed my forehead to the window and looked outside. A map of my village slowly emerged in my mind like a photograph being developed. And as we wound our way through town and the misty mountains above, I became more nervous and my heart started to pound.

Every time we rounded a curve in the road, we could see the "Twin Peaks" in the distance. Those two mountains of exactly the same size, sitting pertly side by side with an outcrop at the summit of each that painted a mental image of a woman lying on her back. Between the two mountains there was also a famous spot where you could bungee jump, plummeting down into the canyon below while being flanked by those enormous breasts. "Welcome to Bungee Jump Valley!" said the shocking-pink flags that lined the narrow mountain road with a width that could accommodate only one vehicle at a time.

As I got off the bus, I flashed the driver a flip card that read "Thank you very much". Then I started to walk in the direction of my mother's house, passing by those shocking-pink signs with the bran vase tucked tightly under my arm as several drops of rain started to fall from the grey sky above.

Needing to pee along the way, I crouched down in some roadside bushes. There was no need to worry about being spotted. After all, there were less than five thousand people living in my village and you almost never ran into anybody on one of these mountain paths. So my only spectator was a tiny tree frog that watched me pee, jumped onto my finger and hopped down onto my palm.

Bidding farewell to the tree frog, I continued along the mountain path lined with cedars, noticing a squirrel scurry by with its fluffy tail held high. The Twin Peaks were close now and I felt another shiver run through my body as I approached my mother's house. I stood out in front for a moment, with the bran vase under one arm and my basket on the other, and looked on at the house that other people in the village referred to as "Ruriko Palace", after my mother. It was a large house and the same property was also home to Amour – a bar my mother ran – as well as a storage hut and several fields. It was a place filled with layers and layers of memories for me, like an intricate *millefeuille*.

By the front gate was a palm tree that must have been planted some time after I'd left. But it seemed ill suited to the mountain climate, leaning heavily to one side and with brown leaves at its base. I gazed across the breadth of the property – the only levelled land in the whole forest – which had originally been owned by my mother's lover, Neocon. The house had been designed to look luxurious. But now the sheen had worn off, it just looked like a cheaply built structure with a dirty grey exterior that made it seem as if it had been showered with ashes from above. If I could take a bulldozer and tear the whole place to the ground, I would.

Neocon was the president of the Negishi Tsuneo Concrete Company, which was very well known in the local area. Apparently, Neocon had been his nickname since elementary school. As for me, I was born to a single mother and never knew who my father was, but I desperately wanted to believe it wasn't him.

I sneaked past the main house, past Bar Amour, and headed to the fields out back. I knew my mother didn't trust the banks, so she kept her money hidden in a champagne bottle, which she buried back there. I'd only come to know about it because I'd once caught her burying it in the middle of the night. But if I could find it, then I could run off with it and start my life anew.

As I stepped across the soil, hailstones started to fall from the grey skies above. I noticed vegetables growing from the soil, which surprised me since Mum had never taken any interest in farming whatsoever. Perhaps she'd got one of her other lovers to work the field. There were potatoes, green onions, Japanese radishes and carrots, and though it was neither the time nor the place to think about it, this array of fresh vegetables gave me a sudden urge to cook.

When I reached a scarecrow that looked somehow out of place, I started to dig at its base. Most people would never dream of burying their money in such an obvious spot. But then, my mum wasn't like most people. After several minutes of pushing through the soil I succeeded only in digging up an old treasure box that I'd buried myself many years before. At first I didn't recognize it because it was covered in dirt, but as I wiped off the mud I recognized the familiar biscuit tin. With a hint of fear, I carefully opened the lid to find a rusty interior crammed with memorable items I'd long since forgotten. There was my favourite water pistol I used to carry with me all the time – the one I used to fill with juice so I could squirt it into my mouth whenever I got thirsty, or fill with water so I could shower the turtle I'd once taken home from a festival. There was a yo-yo I'd often played with when there was nothing better to do, letting it go up, down, up, down, from my perch on the branch of my favourite fig tree. There was a white stone with the word "MUM" written on it that had been important to me as a kind of stress-relieving tool. I'd throw it against the concrete ground to release my frustration and anger whenever my mum had told me off, and on the back of it was a childish sketch of her, with eyes, a nose and a crude mouth scrawled in clumsy crayon. There was also a little stuffed panda, a gold wrapper from the first piece of imported chocolate I ever ate, a scented eraser, a butterfly wing I found on the street, a piece of snake skin and the shells of clams I'd eaten. It was a biscuit tin filed with previously precious things, all of which had long since lost their value to me, and I stood there in a daze wondering what on earth to do with them.

When I closed my eyes, various memories came back to me. Whether I was eating a snack, eating dinner, watching TV, doing homework, taking a bath or sleeping, I'd always been alone, while my mum had always kept herself busy, flaunting her sex appeal and entertaining the customers at Bar Amour. For a moment, I felt like playing with my old yo-yo again. But before I could, there was a loud bang by the door of the main house and a round white blob suddenly came rushing towards me. It was a pig! The same one I'd seen on my mother's New Year's cards every year. And it was charging towards me with the power of a raging bull. Before I could even let out a gasp, the pig was already right in front of me. My mum had been sharing her house with that porcine lodger ever since I'd left home. It was a lot bigger than I'd expected, and really quite intimidating when you saw it up close.

I turned and ran for my life. But the pig was a lot faster than I'd expected and I ended up tripping on vegetable roots several times as the distance closed between us. At one point, one of my shoes fell off, but I just kept on running. And every time its snout poked me in the bottom, I feared it might gobble me up. They were omnivores, after all, which meant they could eat anything. So why not a human?

Little did I know the worst was yet to come. Only moments later, alerted by the sounds of my panic, my mother came running out of the house yelling, "Thief! Thief!" She was dressed in a lace teddy and black rubber boots and had probably not been in bed long after finishing up her night shift at the bar. But scariest of all, she had a sickle in her hand and she didn't seem to recognize me at all! As she ran across the field, ten years older and without make-up, she looked like a middle-aged transvestite who'd had a bit of work done. And as she got closer, I could make out the scent of her sickly sweet perfume that mingled with the smells of the soil and it made me want to vomit.

Luckily she wasn't entirely blind. Just as she was about to bring the sickle down on me she finally recognized me, leading us both to freeze in place in stunned silence. Funnily enough, the first thing I noticed was my mother's breasts. She wasn't wearing a bra and they were clearly visible through the thin material of her teddy. But after all these years, they were still great breasts. Just like those famous Twin Peaks I'd seen from the road.

As I stood staring at my mother with my mouth gaping open, having momentarily forgotten about the flip cards in my basket, she stood staring back at me – her shoulders heaving with her breath that came out in dragon-like puffs of mist. Then, after locking eyes for several moments, she simply turned and walked back to the house, pausing only to gesture for the pig to follow, which it did with tiny steps and a wave of its spiral tail.

It was an absolute worst-case scenario. I'd failed to find her stash of money, but she'd succeeded in finding me, and now my clothes were all covered in mud too. My dream of starting anew somewhere had suddenly evaporated and I didn't even have enough money to take the next minibus back to the terminal. So there was only one place I could go. I put the tin of treasures back into the hole I'd dug earlier and covered it with dirt. Then I retrieved my shoe, picked up grandmother's vase and my basket, brushed myself down and prepared to meet my maker.

As I strode towards the house, I could taste dirt in my mouth. I thought of how it had been ten years since I'd called this place home. Then I looked over to a massive pen by the side of the house, to the place where the pig called Hermes called home, with its big painted name-plate above.

24

After taking a bath, I sipped on my mum's lukewarm and slightly sour coffee and wrote my conversation in pen on the back of one of her flyers. I'd changed into a pair of pyjamas she'd lent me that still carried the heavy scent of her perfume. And for some reason, rather than answering directly to me, my mum decided to reply to me by writing on the back of the flyer in a pen of a different colour, which reminded me of what nice penmanship she had. Mine, on the other hand, was dismal. And being tired and nervous made it worse, leading me to cringe as I scrawled down tiny odd-shaped letters that looked like drowning worms.

We moved over to the *kotatsu*, where we sat facing each other, still conversing entirely in writing. There was a huge expanse of time that had grown between her and I. Like a mountain made of years, with a summit so high that it hurt to try and see it.

Since the bottom line of my situation was that I was broke, I tried asking my mum for a loan. But as I'd expected, she shot me down immediately. She wasn't so cold-hearted that she could let her daughter sleep on the street though. So, in return for promising to take care of Hermes, she agreed to let me move back in – as long as I paid for my food, utilities and rent, of course, which would require me to find another job.

Looking for a job, however, was not going to be such an easy thing. After all, this was a really secluded village with

25

an ageing population. There was probably even a waiting list for that stupid bungee-jump job. But then the idea hit me. I could borrow the storage hut and use it to open a small café. Though we all referred to it as the storage hut, it was actually one of Neocon's model homes that he'd had brought here after some building project had ended. But it was a solid structure with a lot of space inside and far too good to be used only for storage.

It seemed like a good idea. There weren't any other jobs I could really do, after all. But I knew that I could cook. I was confident about that. Maybe this would be the way in which I'd finally get to cook for people and to settle down in this quiet little village. I'd lost everything else I'd ever owned. But I still had my body and all the secrets my grandmother had taught me, and my tongue remembered everything – the fried butterbur with pickled plums, the cooked burdock with vinegar, the assorted sushi full of vegetables, the steamed egg hotchpotch served with broth, the milk pudding made with only egg whites, the steamed buns flavoured with soybean flour, and many other dishes besides.

All of my experiences at the coffee shop, the pub, the kebab shop, the organic restaurant, the popular café and finally the Turkish restaurant – they were all engraved on my body, in my blood, on my flesh, my nails. Just like the rings of a tree. I'd been stripped of everything and left standing vulnerable and naked. But as long as I knew how to cook, I knew I had a chance.

Timidly, I wrote my request and handed it to my mother.

Please Mum, if I promise to work very hard, please will you let me use the storage hut?

Then I placed both hands on the tatami mat and gave her a deep, respectful bow.

Fine. As long as you promise not to give up halfway. She wrote. *You must finish what you start.*

Mum read my eyes as I read her reply. Then she gave a yawn, got up and headed off to bed. This is how I came to be a chef in this quiet mountain village, with my mother loaning me the money to cover opening costs and setting the interest rate so high it would make a loan shark splutter. But I'd carried the dream of having my own place for so long. And I'd carried the hurt of having lost everything. But, because of everything that had happened, I was about to take a big leap forward. A leap I wouldn't have dared to imagine just one day before.

I went to my old room, expecting everything to have been rearranged. But to my surprise, everything was exactly where I'd left it. So I opened a drawer in my dresser, took out a jogging suit and changed into it. It was a maroon suit with a white stripe running down either side and I was happy to fit into it after ten years had passed, although it was now a little bit snug.

I carried the bran vase to the kitchen and set it down where it was cool and the air circulation was good. Mum's kitchen was still the disaster zone it had always been, with soap scum around the sink, bits of decaying food stuck in the sponge, rubbish bins with all the different types of garbage all carelessly mixed together, and the dining table covered in empty instant-noodle cups. You'd never find any of this in my grandmother's kitchen!

I took a peek into one of the kitchen drawers, finding a withered old bag of dried seaweed. Pretending not to see it, I stuffed it back in and closed the drawer. It was a sight that normally would have disgusted me. But in this instance, it somehow made me feel warm and soft inside. I guess I hadn't really understood until that moment how relieved I was to know that my grandmother's bran vase was safe. It had been something she'd held on to through-out her life and, through all the stress that had washed over me recently, I hadn't fully realized the significance of saving it. As a child, I used to lean in and take a good look inside that vase, prompting my grandmother proudly to describe how this vase had survived the great earthquake and even the war. My grandmother had been born in the Taisho era and the vase had been handed down to her from her mother, which meant it must have been in the family at least since the Meiji era or even the Edo period. So it wasn't something you could ever replace. It was a unique and magical bed where vegetables rested happily until ready to emerge transformed as culinary delights.

Ever since the vase had been handed down to me, I'd taken care of its contents by carefully mixing in tangerine peel with the bonito flakes and dried sardines I'd used to make the broth for miso soup. I'd even give it a small glass of beer or a morsel of bread from time to time to encourage more lactic acid production. Grandmother once told me that every one of us produces a slightly different type of lactic acid. Apparently women produced better lactic acid than men, and the best kind of lactic acid could be found on the palms of women who have just given birth. Remembering her many stories, I lifted the lid off the vase once more and breathed in the air from inside. Its scent reminded me of her.

For a while, I sat by the window waiting for the rains to clear. Then I went for a walk around the neighbourhood. My mind was already buzzing with several ideas for my new restaurant and there was no time to be wasted by sleeping. But my mind felt so alive, I don't think I could have slept anyway. There was also a tree I really wanted to go and see.

I wound my way along a familiar mountain trail, then I sprinted up the hill to the favourite spot that held so many fond memories for me. There was an incredibly large fig tree there. And though I'd never once missed my mother in all the ten years since I'd left home, there'd been many occasions when I'd missed that tree. In fact, I'd even had dreams about it.

There was only one place where I could really open my heart. It wasn't when I was with my mum or when I was with my classmates. It was only when I was surrounded by the rich nature of the mountains. I tried climbing the tree for old time's sake. At the age of twenty-five, I was now much heavier than I was back then. But with a bit of a struggle, I still managed to climb up. It seemed the years had changed the tree as well – with its bark that had grown thicker and its branches that had become more sturdy – but somehow I felt it remembered me and was as pleased to see me as I was it.

I pressed my ear against the bark, feeling its warmth. The tree was adorned with fruit the colour of jade, like the baubles on some magnificent Christmas tree. Then I reached out my hand and pressed a finger against the fruits, feeling their firm bodies, like the body of a small child curled up in a ball. I looked up to the sky, seeing a thin layer of clouds like the translucent inner skin of an onion. Then I gazed at the other trees and the grass all around me, sparkling fresh from a gentle shower of rain.

I stood there for a moment, running my fingers through my hair and thinking how the forest hadn't changed one

bit. Then I felt a compulsion to do something transfor-
mational. Taking a pair of scissors from my pocket, I
placed a finger over my fringe as a guide, and watched
them fall away from my body. Then I grabbed a hold
of the hair on the sides and back of my head and began
chopping away again, taking bigger and bigger locks at
a time. I wanted to feel lighter – even if only by a mil-
ligram. Then I let the hair sit in the palm of my hand
until the breeze took it dancing in the air for a moment
before letting it fall to the ground. I brushed back my
short hair with my hand and kept on cutting, feeling it
getting lighter and lighter all the time. I was a chef and
chefs didn't need long hair. And in no time at all, those
locks of hair that had reached halfway to my waist were
all gone, leaving little that extended beyond my collar.

I climbed up and sat in the tree with my new hairdo,
dangling my feet from the branches and looking out over
those Twin Peaks. Then I heard a voice from below.

"Hey there!" the voice called out. I looked down through
the large fig leaves and found an old friend standing below
me dressed in beige workman's clothes. He had rough,
stony features that made him look a little intimidating. But
I knew he was blessed with a kind heart. Rumour had it
that his name was Kumakichi. But everyone just called him
Kuma for short. He worked at an elementary school for a
while back when I was a student and he was something of a

31

hero to all the kids – shovelling snow off the paths in winter so we could get to school, making all the preparations for sports day, and replacing the windows every time one of us children sent a ball smashing through one.

"Ringo? Is that you?" he called out.

Instantly, I felt a distinctly sour feeling. I'd always hated that dreadful nickname bestowed on me by my mother. She once told me she'd called me Rinko because I was the product of a *furin* – an affair with a married man. But because of the way things were pronounced in my local accent, that name soon became Ringo, meaning apple, which was a bit better.

"You've grown so much!" called out Kuma, stepping forwards until he was directly underneath me. "You've grown more beautiful too!"

I fumbled to take the flip cards from my bag in a hurry, flipped to the last one and held it up for him to see.

I have temporarily lost my voice.

Kuma took out his reading glasses from his chest pocket and looked at the card, but either the letters were too small for him to read or he couldn't make sense of them, because he looked up at me with a puzzled expression.

"Yamane," he said, with a confused expression, as if struggling to remember something.

I jumped down off the fig tree and sat down, cross-legged, next to him. The warm autumn sun showered down on our faces like water from a sprinkler and it was hard to believe there had just been a storm.

Yamane.

I remember a day when I was crying so hard, but I don't remember why. I was alone in the school hallway, sobbing my eyes out, when Kuma happened to pass by and call my name. Then he took me by piggyback to the caretaker's office, which was normally off limits to the children. I remember thinking how big and warm his back seemed. It was an entirely new feeling to me since there were never any men in our house.

When we reached the caretaker's office, it was dimly lit and there was a distinct smell to it too. There were all sorts of tools us kids weren't allowed to handle and the kettle on the stove was spurting white steam. Kuma took a saucepan from the shelf and gently brought it over to where I was standing all stiff and nervous.

"Ringo, do you know what this is?" he asked. Then slowly he opened the lid to reveal a small creature the colour of chestnuts inside.

"It's a Yamane," he said.

"A Yamane?" I asked, looking up at him with teary eyes. Then his face crumpled into a kind smile as he gently picked it up and placed it on my hand. Amazingly, the little dormouse didn't move. It just kept on sleeping. And without even realizing, I had stopped crying.

I hadn't thought of that day for a long time, but it all came back to me so vividly. It was almost as if I could still feel the Yamane on my palm. That was the day we'd first become friends and we'd remained good friends ever since. I took the flip cards back from him and flipped to another page.

How are you?

I handed the card to him and he nodded several times. Then he started to tell me about all the different things that had happened in the village, and to him, during the time I'd been away.

Kuma had got married during my time in the city, to a lady from Argentina. He told me, with a sparkle in his eyes, how nice she was; how beautiful. And he told me that she was his *siñorita*. I wasn't sure if he meant to say she was his *señorita*, but it certainly sounded like *siñorita* to me. She was a lot younger than Kuma and, after getting married, they'd moved in with his mother. He told me they'd soon been blessed with a child, as he took out a photo of a lovely little girl with big sparkling eyes. But unfortunately the marriage hadn't lasted long. The relationship between Kuma's mother and Siñorita had soon turned sour. And one day, Siñorita – who had always been a city girl at heart – moved away from the village, taking their daughter with her. Kuma, on the other hand, was like a country mountain to his very core. His family had lived off the land for generations and he knew everything about the mountains around him, but little of what lay beyond. He didn't know how he would live if he were to move away from his home town and he knew he couldn't leave his elderly mother behind. So instead, he gave up on chasing after his beloved Siñorita and stayed where he was in this little village nestled in the mountains, living a lonely life with only his ageing mother and a mature female goat for company.

Standing up, Kuma took out a couple of chestnuts from his breast pocket and handed them to me. They were round and shiny, and when I rolled them around in my palm they made a sound like a castanet. I took out the flip cards from my basket again and showed another to Kuma.

Thank you very much.

He gave me a smile that seemed to say "It's nothing". Then he turned and walked away, his big back swaying as he walked along the narrow mountain path and his left leg dragging behind, weakened by an old wound sustained in a battle with a big black bear. One of his many tales.

"Soak the chestnuts in *shochu* and it'll do wonders for the cuts," called out Kuma with a turn of his head and a flash of the same smile I'd seen when he first showed me that Yamane. I got up and walked over to a nearby stream. Since I'd cut my hair with such gusto, but no mirror, I had no idea what it looked like. So I nervously knelt on the grass at the water's edge, leant over to take a look at my reflection, and was surprised to see the short-haired girl staring back at me. It still looked like me, but a very different me. I tried to run my fingers through my hair, like I did when it was long. But they quickly passed through and into thin air. But it wasn't bad. I felt lighter. Like egg whites whipped into meringue. I scooped some water up in my palms and carried it to my mouth. It tasted so pure and soft. Then I rearranged my hair with my wet hands, stood up and drank in the sight of the light that came down through the fig leaves to dance at the bottom of the stream.

I decided to take a leisurely walk into the village. But as I began to stroll down the road to the bus stop, my steps were interrupted every ten minutes or so by a piercing scream. At first I imagined something dreadful must have happened. Then I realized they were coming from the direction of the bungee-jump canyon.

As I strolled along, I could see praying mantis on the leaves, chocolate vines and garden burnets. All of them unchanged. I noticed the local inns and B&Bs that had grown more dirty and a little rustier on the outside. But I could see from the towels hanging by their windows that they were nevertheless still in business. I passed by a Jizo statue at the side of the road that was wearing a

new bib as it stood by a colourful bunch of chrysanthe-
mums in an improvised vase fashioned from an empty
sake bottle. I passed by the riverside public baths, by the
run-down strip club. And by the vending machines in the
arcade. They were all sights that filled me with a sense of
nostalgia. But at the same time, I wanted to smash them
all with my fist.

I crossed the road and cut through a shopping arcade
with a few shops dotted along it and patches of blue sky
peeking in through the holes that peppered its rusty roof-
ing. This had once been the thriving business district of
a popular hot spring resort. Hot springs used to be such
big business, attracting tourists from all over the country
whenever a new one was discovered. But the transportation involved in getting here had never been great, and
for the busloads who did make it this far, there was never
enough accommodation. So it wasn't long before enthusiasm for our hot springs cooled.

Though it was the middle of the day, most of the shops
had their shutters down. It reminded me of a plastic doll
my grandmother used to have. When I turned it on its
side, it let out a small sound and closed its eyelids, but they
never shut completely. Just like those shop shutters, they
remained open just a touch at the bottom. But despite all
the shops looking so tired, run-down and closed up, there
were doubtless still people living inside them.

I looked at each shop as I walked along slowly, following the sweet smell of cakes drifting out of the only confectioner's in the village. Strawberry cakes and savarins were lined up inside the shop's foggy display counter and I remembered how my mum used to come home drunk and shove spoonfuls of the shop's puddings into my mouth, even though I was already sleeping. I wondered if the next generation of the family had taken over the shop by now. There seemed to be a different woman standing behind the counter, after all.

Next door to the cake shop, there used to be a small *tonkatsu* shop serving deep-fried breaded pork cutlets. Only now it was closed down, with a poster taped to the shutter written in ballpoint pen.

We will be closing the shop for a short while.

From the handwriting, it seemed the message had been scrawled down in a hurry. But on seeing a date from last year written in the corner of the note, I realized their optimism may have been a little hasty. As I continued along the arcade, I saw that the bookshop and the optician's shops had also suffered a similar fate, with the premises of the bookshop now being used for a video-rental business. But it didn't seem to stock the kind of movies you'd go to the cinema to see, judging by the posters of girls in their underwear in the window. Further along the street, the old "Happy Family Planning" vending machine was still standing in the same spot it had always been. And diagonally across from it was the only supermarket in the village that carried a full range of basic everyday items. The supermarket was still quietly doing business. But with a sparse population of customers and its blinking *Supermarket Yorozu* electric sign, it looked like a shop drawing its last breaths of life in a town already on life support.

Nevertheless, it didn't look like I'd have any trouble in getting the ingredients for my restaurant. In the rice paddies, sparkling gold ears of rice dipped their heavy heads, while the mountains sprouted an abundance of fresh vegetables – more than enough for us, even after the livestock had eaten their share. There was fresh water always available at the stream nearby, so there was no need for me to get a filter or to buy bottled water. There were cows, mountain goats and lambs grazing in the pastures, so fresh milk would never be a problem and I could even try my hand at making cheese. A little further out, there were farms with pigs and chickens, taking care of wings, eggs and pork. And since it was the hunting season, I could easily ask the hunters for a share of their catch. Furthermore, even though the village was in the mountains, it was still just a short drive from the ocean, so I could hop into a car any time to go and pick up fresh seafood. On the way back, I could go past the steeper mountain slopes on the other sides with their grapevines that produced pretty decent wine. The village also put its fresh water and rice to good use in the production of all kinds of great sake and I was sure there must be plenty of farms growing fruit and herbs as well. It seemed as if everywhere you looked in the village, there were people hard at work making wonderful food. For the only things that weren't so easy to come by in the village, such as good olive oil and other special ingredients, I could simply order them online. Of course, I would have to pay for using Mum's Internet connection.

So there I was, surrounded by mountains, the ocean, rivers and fields – all treasure troves of ingredients. From a culinary perspective, it was so much better than being in the city. In fact, it was almost too good to be true. Everything around me was filling my mind with ideas for my new restaurant, painting colourful marble patterns in my head. I looked up and saw the sun about to set below the corner of the rolling green hills – a smooth dark orange ball, like the yolk of a freshly laid egg. Until now, I'd always thought the sunsets in the city were so beautiful, with the sun slowly sinking between the tall buildings. But this sunset was simply magnificent; a true masterpiece of Mother Nature. If only everyone could see such beauty. Maybe then they would never dream of carving up nature for their own convenience. I looked down to see the long shadow that stretched out from my body, telling me that the night was creeping in from somewhere deep inside the forest. So I ran home along the cobblestone path, determined to get there before the darkness could engulf me, but just after my mum had left for Bar Amour.

I realized I'd been awake for more than twenty-four hours before I got to sleep that night. I was absolutely exhausted and in a very deep sleep when the call of an owl woke me. In my tiredness, I'd forgotten to close the curtains and from my bed I could see a single, solitary star sparkling beyond the frame of the window. It was such a tiny, dwindling light; one that might go out if I was to sneeze in its direction.

At first I didn't recognize the voice of Grandpa Owl. It had been ten years since I'd left the village, so surely there was no way he could still be alive. But there he was. I glanced at the clock and felt a shiver run down my spine. He was here, still alive, and calling out at the stroke of midnight. I counted the hoots. There were exactly twelve, just as I'd expected. Grandpa Owl lived in the attic of the main house. Ever since I was a child, I remember how he'd given twelve hoots on the stroke of midnight without fail. Not once did he ever miss a day, and his hoots were so precise and regular that it was as if he had his own metronome. It was probably at that time that I'd started to become impressed by the ability of animals. Even Mum had a soft spot for Grandpa Owl. She believed he was the guardian of our house and I believed that too. But nobody had ever seen him, which made him that bit more special.

Ten years ago I'd wandered away from this house and today I'd wandered back with a broken heart. For all that time, Grandpa Owl had been here, going on with his daily work. He was right up there at the top of my list of people and creatures I respected and I felt somehow safe to have him watching over me. Now that I think about it, I remember how I used to feel lonely at night as a child, and how I used to feel safe enough to go to sleep as long as I pictured Grandpa Owl in the attic. I shut my eyes and imagined I was a child again, bathing in the peace of his presence, until eventually, after such a long and memorable chain of events, my incredibly long day came to a soothing, warm conclusion.

From that day on, the days zoomed by like the duck hawks that glided through the canyon between the Twin Peaks. I'd always been kept busy by my many part-time jobs in the past, but I'd never been this busy in the whole twenty-five years of my life! Of course, it wasn't like I was so busy that I never had time to think about my boy-friend. I did think of him from time to time. But because I was so very busy, there was just never any time for me to linger on those thoughts. Every day, I'd start out early by caring for Hermes the pig, which consisted of following the detailed rules and guidelines about food and other things lovingly put together in the Hermes logbook by my mum. Sometimes her comments made me laugh, like the one that said, "Don't give Hermes too much food or she'll make a pig of herself." To my mum, Hermes was obviously much more than just a pig.

I'd always assumed Mum had given the pig that name since she'd always been a fan of big-name fashion brands. But instead the name was actually derived from "L-Mes", with the "L" standing for her breed, Landrace, and the other part sounding a little like "Miss" since she was a female. According to Mum's notebook, Landrace pigs were originally bred in Denmark for bacon to go along with the eggs the British so loved for breakfast. They have a small head and a long torso and they're also very intelligent. But what mainly distinguishes them from other breeds such as the Large Yorkshire or Medium Yorkshire is their long face and droopy ears.

Her name may have played a part in forming the impression, but Hermes seemed to me to have quite an elegant face. Pigs are known to be quite clean animals and Hermes was certainly no exception. She had a place in her pen for eating and a place for going to the bathroom and she never mixed the two. According to her logbook, she'd arrived at my mum's place when she was four weeks old.

Mother pigs usually have fourteen nipples and the babies immediately decide which nipple belongs to whom, with the strongest pig getting the nipple that produces the most milk and the weakest runt getting the least milk, causing him or her to get even weaker still. In Japanese we call those weak ones *hinebuta*. Hermes had been one of those too. She'd weighed only a kilogram at birth and just a little over three kilograms when she'd first arrived, which was way below average. If it hadn't been for Mum intervening, little Hermes would have wound up with an early appointment in the butcher's shop.

I don't know if her lack of nutrition as a piglet had anything to do with it, but Hermes didn't go into heat even after reaching adolescence at four months old. She just continued to live here with Mum, never mating, never producing offspring. She had her own field out back of the house, from where you could recognize the distinct smell of her droppings. This was the magic fertilizer that gave Mum's vegetables their special shine. Not that she gave a damn about the things people eat. But when it came to Hermes, only organic would do. All those vegetables out back were free from pesticides and chemical fertilizers and Hermes's main food was a vegetable-based mix including natural corn and soy – none of that genetically modified stuff. Most outrageous of all was the wild yeast bread Mum fed Hermes for dessert after breakfast every day. It was handmade and delivered from a famous bakery in Tokyo. But the diet seemed to work wonders for Hermes. She had a shiny coat, an impressive tail with a perfectly formed curl, and a smiling expression that made her appear to be in a state of permanent satisfaction. If only I had enough money to buy bread like that. Until then, I'd have to be content with baking my own bread.

One day, Kuma came by to give me a bag of sweet-and-sour apples that had just ripened. I knew he kept his garden free of chemicals too, and I used the apples to make my own yeast. Then I'd make my own dough, kneading it at night before shaping it and baking it when I awoke in the morning to a symphony of birdsong. It was hard work, but I'd always enjoyed baking. So once it became part of my daily routine, it really wasn't bad at all.

At first, Hermes turned her nose up at the bread I baked for her. I wasn't sure if it was the taste, the shape or the ingredients. But she clearly noticed that something was different. It was disheartening to see something I'd made being left uneaten. The fact that the disgruntled customer was a pig didn't help either. So I set out to rework the recipe in a way that would meet her approval. Mum's logbook mentioned that Hermes liked nuts, so I tried putting acorns into the bread. And as soon as I did that, she started eating away. So I started to mix in different nuts I found in the forest and in no time she started to grow on me.

Hermes weighed more than a hundred kilograms. Sometimes as I'd watch her rounded body munching away on the bread, I'd feel like I was watching a sister. Of course, I didn't like the way Mum showered Hermes with affection, but I wasn't at all jealous of Hermes. I just pulled on my rubber boots and set about cleaning the pig pen. Adult pigs get overheated easily, so I'd open the roof to let in a breeze for her when the weather was warm. Then, in the winter, we added acrylic boards to help keep the heat in, but even then we'd take them off at least once a day to stop the air from going stagnant inside. The floor of her pen was covered in sawdust and wheat husks, which I gathered up with the pig manure every morning and carried in a bucket to the compost heap in the field. Then I'd rush through my own breakfast and begin my preparations for the opening of the eatery. I'd decided it would be an eatery from the start. Not a café, not a bar, not an *izakaya*, but an eatery.

Every day there was so much to be done. One day, I made tablecloths by sewing together old scraps of material. I'd spent another day going into town to find the kind of chairs I wanted to use. Using Mum's computer, I'd ordered the cutlery I wanted online. And all this time I didn't speak to anyone. I just wrote things down or used hand gestures to explain myself. It was such an extremely busy time. But such an exhilarating one too.

I was fortunate to have Kuma around, who was always willing to lend a hand. He knew everyone in the village and everything about nature from having lived here for so long, so he was an important adviser to me. Whenever I ran into difficulties, all I had to do was tell him and in most cases the issue would be quickly resolved. He also helped me finish off all the interior work, doing the heavy lifting, cutting wood, hammering planks together and using the chainsaw while I painted the walls, waxed the floor and set the tiles. As we worked together, ideas kept coming to my mind for other ways to make improvements and though we worked from morning to night, we were still a long way from nearing completion.

As we continued to work, the trees in the mountains changed colour just a shade every day and the hours of sunlight began to dwindle. I wanted to turn my eatery into a mysterious space – one that would feel both familiar and completely new to anyone stepping into it for the first time. Like a secret cave in which you could find yourself.

After about a month of heavy work, the eatery was coming close to the way I'd envisioned it. We'd put cork boards on the floor with terracotta tiling on top. We'd got a thick rug in preparation for the arrival of winter. And in the middle of the room was a solid antique-style table made by Kuma's father, a carpenter, just before he'd passed away. Its chestnut wood was a beautiful faded shade of golden brown and the table had a unique design that was neither eastern nor western. The chairs that accompanied it had come from a second-hand shop in town – small wooden chairs with woven-rope seats. They looked as if they'd originally come from a music hall, and with a dash of Turkish blue paint I'd transformed them into something quite charming.

The walls were a nice shade of natural orange, close to the colour of egg yolk. We'd achieved that particular shade by going over the wood with natural ingredients and Kuma had asked a foreign artist, who happened to be staying in the village, to paint Kannon – the goddess of mercy – on the wall, with angel-like wings spreading up to the ceiling. It was a painting done in light strokes and it rather reminded me of the work of Cocteau. I especially loved the firewood stove that Kuma managed to get from a closed-down junior high school in the neighbouring village. But my favourite item had been given to us by Kuma's neighbour. It was a handmade chandelier from the Taisho period with indentations for candles to be placed inside.

Though I only actually needed a dining table, I also wanted a sofa bed where anyone who got sleepy after eating or any drivers who'd fancied a drink or two could lie down for a while. I also liked the idea of having a place in the eatery where I could sleep in case I got into a fight with Mum and had to stay away for a little while. I grabbed hold of a few wine crates I'd got from a whole-saler near town and Kuma had helped by driving them back. Then I'd put them together in the shape of a sofa bed and covered them with a small floral-patterned futon. I used the same material to make some cushion covers too, and placed them on the bed together with a tartan blanket.

In the bathroom, I covered the walls with tiles, using different-coloured pieces to make a mosaic of a couple of birds. It looked a little primitive, but in a way that I liked, which was great because a bad bathroom environment can ruin a customer experience, no matter how good the food might be. I even spent some extra money on getting the latest electric Washlet for the toilet seat, and together with the little window in the bathroom wall, the room became quite a nice, relaxing space.

I fashioned a pathway from the village road with pebbles I'd found in the river, spelling out the word *Welcome* at the end of the path in different-coloured stones. Along the sides of the eatery we planted my favourite raspberries, blueberries and wild berry bushes. I also asked a local plaster shop to crush old ceramic roof tiles and mix them in with cement to make a deep-pink plaster for the outer wall, which I decorated by embedding seashells from a nearby beach. The door, which can make or break a person's first impression of a restaurant, I purchased in an online auction. Of course, Neocon's original house had a door too, but it was made of aluminium and simply didn't match the look I was trying to go for. Instead I chose a smoky-dark-brown French-style door shaped like an upside-down U and used a piece of metal I'd picked up in the mountains that looked kind of like a lizard for the doorknob. I was very pleased with the space Kuma and I had managed to put together in such a relatively short time. Now all that was left was to finish the interior, which I could do bit by bit after the actual opening.

Thanks to Kuma, my kitchen turned out much better than I'd imagined, and I quickly moved my grandmother's bran vase into it from my mum's dirty kitchen. The most important thing for me was for the kitchen to be light, clean and easy to use. I use the fewest tools possible when cooking, so I didn't need a dishwasher, a microwave or a rice cooker. The only things I absolutely needed were a refrigerator, a sink, a gas stove and an oven, all of which I was able to pick up for cheap from a nearby Chinese restaurant that had just gone out of business. The sink was as good as new, and luckily it was the perfect height for my short stature. For the extractor hood, we improvised something using an old bucket, which looked kind of silly, but nice in a quirky sort of way. We also tore down the whole eastern wall and put a large plate of glass in its place, allowing the brilliant natural light to flood in while I cooked. Kuma made the joists for the ceiling using locally cut trees and from them I dangled baskets made of mountain twine. From the other door of the kitchen, I could walk right out into the herb garden I'd planted. I took a moment to drink in the sight. I'd worked in many kitchens during my years, but this was by far the best.

With the money I borrowed from Mum, I bought a set of professional knives and other essential utensils. There was even enough left over to get some really great dishes, bowls and other things and Mum gave me an entire set of dishes that I'd found in the back of one of her cupboards. They'd been given to her by Grandmother and they included such wonderful pieces – colourful cups from the Taisho and Victorian eras, old Vietnamese bowls depicting the fall of the Annam state, Imari-ware bean dishes, white Richard Ginori soup bowls and even a set of Baccarat champagne glasses with a discontinued design. On the underside of each piece was a sticker with my grandmother's handwriting on it explaining a little about its history. Mum gave these things to me as an opening-day gift. And though I knew they were little more than junk to her, they were treasures to me.

I have a theory that female personalities are passed down from generation to generation, flipping one way and then back with each addition to the lineage. Being brought up by such a down-to-earth woman, my mother had grown up to lead a roller-coaster life. Brought up by my mum, I'd grown up to lead a life a little more down to earth again. It was like an eternal game of Othello.

I decided to store these precious dishes in the tea-ceremony chest I'd found lying in storage. Just a wipe of a cloth had brought its surfaces beautifully back to life, so I placed them directly below the window through which my customers could gaze at the Twin Peaks as they ate. By now, I was counting the days to the official opening.

One day, Kuma visited me on a tricycle. It was an electric tricycle for adults and was useful for transporting heavy things. I'm sure there's a proper name for this type of special tricycle, but I don't know it. There were two tyres on the back and a big basket. There was even a rear-view mirror.

"This is a gift for you, Ringo," he said. "I gave it to Siñorita a long time ago, but she has no use for it now. Would you like to use it?" Then he grabbed hold of the Turkish-blue paint pot and asked me if he could use some of it. And before I could say anything, he began painting a layer of blue on the slightly rusted tricycle. Though I tapped him on the back many times and waved my hands in the air to tell him I couldn't possibly accept something with such sentimental value, he carried on regardless until I had before me a new-looking tricycle with a gleam of brilliant blue.

"So, are you going to call this place Amour?" asked Kuma.

"No way!" I thought, and waved my hands in the air frantically. I'd been so busy with everything that I'd forgotten one of the most important things – the name! But of course I didn't want to call it Amour, not after all the work Kuma and I had put into creating such a unique place.

That night in bed, I gave a lot of thought to what I was going to call the place. And as I lay there listening to Grandpa Owl at midnight, it came to me – The Snail. That was it! The perfect name! And with that, I snapped my fingers with a muffled sound from beneath the futon covers, in which I was wrapped up like a rolled cake.

The next morning I called Kuma on his mobile phone. I still couldn't talk, but I'd at least developed a system where I played music we'd agree on beforehand if I wanted him to come over. Kuma chose Matsuda Seiko's 'Nagisa Balcony'. Apparently, this was the song his Siñorita used to sing at Bar Amour before she'd left the village, taking their daughter with her. So Kuma made a tape of it and I carried it in my favourite basket, along with a cassette player.

I was surprised how easy it was to live with only limited communication. It certainly wasn't as hard as one might imagine. But then, I'd never been much of a conversationalist and if I imagined I was living alone then there was really nothing to it.

I placed some stones on the ground, spelling out *The Snail*. Then I waited for Kuma to arrive so I could read the expression on his face. He arrived, read the name, then, reading the inquisitive look on my face, he responded, "Very nice." Our communication via facial expression couldn't have been clearer if we'd written our feelings across our faces in marker pen. We were two people completely in sync with each other.

Kuma turned to pick up a paintbrush. Then he dipped it in white paint and wrote THE SNAIL on the plate attached to the blue tricycle basket in confident letters. I loved his handwriting. It was rough and ready. But it was full of love. And from that day on, we referred to the blue tricycle as the Snail Mobile.

I decided to take the Snail Mobile out for a test drive along the paths of our quiet mountain village. I felt a little worried since I didn't have a driver's licence. After all, I'd never needed one in the city. But out here in the country, you need wheels to get around and I couldn't be calling Kuma for every little errand. But thanks to the Snail Mobile, I could get around on my own. So I came to terms with the fact that Kuma had given me something of such sentimental value and I decided to use it and take very good care of it.

Slowly but surely, I trundled along the mountain paths, looking up occasionally at the beautiful autumn sky, with its covering of clouds like skinny jellyfish with impressive tentacles that reached out in every direction. I took a deep breath, filling my lungs with air as a hawk came flying overhead from the direction of the ocean. I watched it let out a cry as it circled above my head, then off it went in the direction of the Twin Peaks. Nature was everywhere.

I came across a mountain grapevine along the way, reaching up, picking a grape and popping it into my mouth. And though it was bitter and sour when eaten fresh, I knew there was something I could do with them. So I grabbed a few handfuls and placed them in my basket before the bears could come and get them. Then I placed my basket safely in the front of the Snail Mobile. I also picked up handfuls of acorns so I could add them to Hermes's bread.

My dream of having my own place was now within reach. Things were still hard work, though. I still trod in Hermes's droppings at least once a day. I still had chestnuts falling on my head. And I still kept tripping over pebbles along the mountain paths and almost falling flat on my face. But the number of moments that filled my heart with joy far outnumbered those I'd felt while living in the city. Even the tiniest little thing had the power to make me feel happy. Like turning over a beetle struggling on its back and watching it walk away. Like feeling the warmth of a freshly laid egg against my cheek. Like seeing a droplet of water balance on a leaf's surface, more beautiful than any diamond. Or like finding a Kinugasa mushroom at the entrance to the bamboo forest, carefully plucking it and taking it home to place in my miso soup, with its wonderful flavour and its underside as beautiful and intricate as hand-knitted lace. All of these things filled me with wonder and gratitude and made me want to kiss God on the cheek.

In my mind, I had a very good idea of how The Snail would be. It would be a little different from other restaurants, serving just one pair of customers each day. I'd talk to the customer the day before, either in person or via fax or email – asking them about the kinds of foods they liked, about their family and about their budget too. Then I'd take all that information and make the best menu possible. Ideally, I'd have the meal starting at about six – long before the sounds of drunken karaoke drifted in from Bar Amour, and giving the customers plenty of time to really enjoy their meal. For the same reason, I was careful not to place a clock in the dining room, relying only on the kitchen timer to mark the passing of the hours. I'd also keep the place smoke-free since smoke could so easily hijack the flavour of the food and I wouldn't play music either – preferring my guests to have the sounds of my cooking and the natural world outside as their soundtrack.

When I got back from running my errands around the village, Kuma was there chopping wood for my firewood stove. So I took out my notebook, wrote down a message for him and waited for him to take a moment's rest.

Please tell me what you would most like to eat.

It felt a little like I was confessing deep feelings for him, and it made me blush. I was afraid in case my hand might be shaking too. But then, this was no spur-of-the-moment offer. I'd been meaning to do this for him for a long time, as a way to thank him for all his help. I had neither the means nor the money to pay him or get him a normal gift. But I had my passion for cooking and a desire to cook for him that came from the bottom of my heart.

Judging by his face, the offer came as a complete surprise. It was as if he'd bitten into something bitter, thinking it would be sweet. Then he cleared his throat and replied.

"What I want to eat…" He mumbled. Then he paused. Then he silently went back to chopping wood as if the question had never been asked.

Several minutes later, he put down his axe and began telling me a story about Siñorita. Thoughts of cooking reminded him of her and of his beloved daughter, and I understood completely. There had been so many small pleasures that had filled my moments here. But there were still so many times when thoughts of my boyfriend would spring back to mind. It was as if there was a wound deep inside me that wouldn't heal. A wound that instead grew deeper with each day. Every now and then, I'd see someone in town who looked like him from a distance and I couldn't stop myself from running after them to get a closer look. To see if it was really him. To see if he'd come back for me. And like one of Pavlov's dogs, the scent of those beautiful exotic spices in my cooking – like the ones I could smell on his skin – would bring tears to my eyes.

Just thinking of cooking was enough to make me feel sad at first. Every time I'd step into the kitchen and wrap the apron about my waist, I'd picture my boyfriend with his dark skin, his shiny white teeth, those sincere eyes and that high-bridged nose. It was as if India and Turkey were two balls of clay, each a different colour. Two balls that had been rolled together tightly into a single ball and sent crushing into my chest, leaving only the void of being cast aside – a void that would never be easy to fill.

As Kuma continued to chop wood, he told me that the first dish Siñorita had ever cooked for him had been curry.

"I pretty much eat whatever the old woman puts on the table nowadays," he added with a distant gaze as if looking to the plains of Argentina, "so it's been a while since I had a curry."

So curry it was. But this was to be no ordinary curry. It was going to be the best curry ever. It was a very sentimental dish for me too. I don't know how many times I must have made it for my Indian boyfriend, and for him curry was soul food.

Once Kuma finished chopping the wood, we sat down to a quick lunch of oven-baked noodles. Then, afterwards, I carefully washed, boiled and soaked the freshly picked mountain grapes in balsamic vinegar. In twelve years, they would be ready to eat and I closed my eyes and imagined how they would taste. It was possible that they might spoil along the way. But it was also possible that I might be standing here in the same kitchen with the same fresh enthusiasm in my heart. And with these prayers in my mind, I carefully poured the balsamic vinegar into the bottles I'd prepared earlier.

When my opening day finally arrived, I stepped out of the house with my chest puffed out and strode over to The Snail, with Hermes – now very friendly with me – crying out to cheer me on. A fine, misty rain had been falling in the village since early morning and I looked up to enjoy it, just like a real snail might.

The sign I'd been working on the previous afternoon was splattered with raindrops. It was on a flat piece of wood cut in the shape of a snail by Kuma and I'd painted *The Snail* on it in yellow paint, with handwriting like that of a preschooler. I gently placed my hand on the sign before taking out the key – the only key in the world – to The Snail. Then I opened the upside-down U-shaped door and listened to its old, wise-sounding creak, as if it had a mind and voice of its own.

Since I was only taking one reservation a day, I hadn't really bothered to advertise. Nevertheless, a delivery man came walking up the path with a huge congratulatory flower garland, just like the ones you see outside of newly opened pachinko parlours. It was from Neocon, who must have heard all about my eatery from Mum. And though I appreciated the thought, it wasn't really in keeping with the rustic, warm atmosphere I was going for, so I picked it up and hid it behind Bar Amour.

I'd been thinking about the curry ever since the day when I'd asked Kuma what he wanted to eat, and planning it had even kept me awake at night on a couple of occasions. I'd asked him for a little more detail on what kind of curry he liked best, but he'd replied, "Just curry," which didn't help at all.

At first, I thought about trying to recreate the curry Siñorita had made for him. But his memory was too foggy to recall enough details. I also knew that no matter what kind of curry I made, it wouldn't taste anywhere near as good as the one Siñorita had made for him. So in the end, I decided to make it my own way. And after a lot more thought, I finally decided to make a pomegranate curry, using fresh pomegranates from a place I knew in the depths of the forest.

I'd first learnt how to make pomegranate curry from an Iranian chef I worked with at the Turkish restaurant. Adding a few handfuls of pomegranate seeds gave the curry a deep, ruby-red colour and a sweet-and-sour taste that made your mouth water. I've never been to Iran, but the taste of that curry had the power to evoke images of Iranian landscapes in sepia colours. For me, it was such a special dish. It was the dish my boyfriend and I had decided we'd put on our own menu when we opened our restaurant so we could be the ones to introduce it to the Japanese.

In preparation, I'd gone up into the mountains the day before and climbed several trees until I'd picked all the pomegranates I needed. It was important to me to use local produce as much as possible in my eatery. But the pomegranate I'd popped in my mouth while sitting up in one of those trees was much more sour and tangy than the ones I was used to. It was a surprise that made my whole body seem to come alive and so much more of an experience than you'd ever get from one of those supermarket pomegranates with their excessive wrapping. These pomegranates were truly wild and waiting in my kitchen for their chance to transform Kuma's curry.

As I lit the firewood stove, I felt overcome with a sense of sanctity. I pulled the strings tight on my new apron, wrapped a cloth around my head and scrubbed my hands carefully with soap. After the day when I cut my hair short in the fig tree, I decided I liked it short and went to the beauty parlour at the edge of the village and asked them to take an electric razor to it. Now I shaved my own head once every three days or so. It just seemed to make sense – now I didn't need to worry about getting hair in the food and I no longer had any desire to make myself attractive in the eyes of others, anyway. I even went so far as to consider shaving off my eyebrows too, but decided not to in the end in case it scared the customers.

Lying on the spotless kitchen counter next to the pome-granates were some onions and beef that looked like they couldn't wait to be cooked. I gently placed my freshly washed hands on them and held them up to my face one at a time, as if cherishing a new life that had entered this world. Then I closed my eyes and exchanged a few words with each one in turn. No one had taught me to do this, but I'd somehow got into the habit of going through this ceremony before starting – lifting each ingredient to my face, enjoying its aroma, asking it how it would like to be cooked and then listening for its voice to tell me. Of course, it may just have been my imagination, but I often felt I really could hear their faint voices. And when I could, I imagined kneeling in my mind to pray to the god of cooking.

Dear God, let me succeed in making a good curry. Let me help these ingredients share their flavours without disappointment, without hurting them and without waste.

Once I felt my prayers had reached the god of cooking, I slowly opened my eyes and lost myself in my culinary world. Almost as soon as I began chopping the onions, tears started to well up in my eyes. So I gritted my teeth, unsure of how many tears were falling for the onion and how many were falling over memories of my boyfriend. But even when the tears came rolling down my cheeks like eggs from a sea turtle on the shore, I still continued to chop. In fact, I cried all the way through making that pomegranate curry. Moments with my boyfriend came one by one from my box of memories – turning into tears and running away. It was only really then that I realized how I'd left the city in such a daze and thrown myself entirely into the making of the eatery, all the while pushing thoughts of my boyfriend down somewhere deep inside. But now, they were all ready to spill out, like cheap colourful handkerchiefs from a magician's pocket – colouring everything before me in shades of nostalgia until I couldn't even tell whether the onions had browned or not. But in less than an hour, the sweet, sour smell of pomegranate curry had already suffused the kitchen.

Late that afternoon, Kuma arrived right on time in his small truck. Until then, I'd only ever seen him wearing his overalls. So when I first saw a figure coming down the path in a suit, I thought that maybe someone from the mob had come for me! Maybe to complain about me setting up business here or for something relating to someone's grudge against Mum. Either of those things would have been entirely possible in the city.

Of course, all fear left my mind the moment I heard Kuma shout out, "Hey there!" in his characteristically relaxed tone. It gave me great pleasure to open the door to The Snail and welcome my first ever guest. Starting today, I was a truly professional chef. In addition to his black suit, Kuma was wearing a bright-red tie and he'd styled his thinning hair in a pompadour. His footwear, however, was familiar. He had the same old rubber boots on, but today they'd been brushed clean of leaves and mud and polished until they were as shiny as a tuna belly laid out at the fish market.

Before taking his seat, Kuma went around the place checking all the work he'd done – making sure the chandelier was hanging right, that there were no bubbles trapped in the terracotta and so forth. I gave him a flash of the "Please Wait" sign I'd put on my apron and hurried back to the kitchen to put the finishing touches to my pomegranate curry. From the kitchen I could see him lighting up a fat cigar. This was supposed to be a non-smoking eatery. But since Kuma was such a special guest, I decided to allow it just this once and passed him an ashtray.

Once I was sure there was just the right amount of salt in my curry, I poured a generous serving over my freshly made buttered rice and carried it swiftly to the table where Kuma awaited. Then I prepared a small side dish of Japanese radish for him, wishing I could lay my hands on some of the shallots I'd pickled back in the summer. Then I placed a wooden spoon by the side of his plate, gave him a deep bow, returned to the kitchen and closed the curtain behind me. All that was left now was for Kuma to enjoy himself.

With the exception of my boyfriend, I felt awkward watching people eating the food I'd prepared for them. I personally found it more embarrassing than if someone were to take a magnifying glass to my nipple or the inside of my vagina. But, on the other hand, I was dying to see Kuma's reaction. So I opened the curtain just a touch and peered through to see him already eating away. Then I used a small hand mirror to catch sight of his expression. Every time I moved it, a small circle of white light danced around his face like a little butterfly, but he didn't seem to mind at all. He just carried on eating his pomegranate curry – without a sound, without an expression, without a

65

single comment. I started to worry about whether he liked it or not and whether any of my tears had accidentally fallen in while making it. The more I thought about it, the more I worried. And the more I worried, the more I thought about it, until I started to wonder if I'd made a big mistake and began to lose the confidence to continue as a professional chef at all!

So there you have it. Enjoying cooking and being a professional chef were two completely different things. By now, I was racked with regrets. I wished I could have chosen a dish that might have suited Kuma's palate better and I wanted to snatch the half-eaten pomegranate from his hands and throw it down the sink. I could so easily have made a curry with pork cutlets, or with a meat patty. I could have even just made one based on a store-bought mild curry roux. I started to go to pieces, even doubting the way the pickled Japanese radishes might taste and wondering if the change in climate for the bran vase might have had some adverse effect on the taste. Had all of this been for nothing? Just pure self-indulgence? But before I had the chance to burst into full-blown tears, Kuma suddenly called out, "Ringo-chan! I've never eaten a curry like this in my life!"

I don't know whether Kuma knew I was standing right behind the curtain, but he seemed to turn precisely in my direction as he said this. What a change a kind comment can make. Just one hour earlier, I'd been crying out of loneliness. Now I was crying for joy.

"I wish Siñorita and my daughter could eat this too," Kuma mumbled. And in my hand mirror, I could see him looking down at the curry with such a happy expression. Following the great success of the pomegranate curry, I felt better as I prepared the American coffee for after the meal. It's kind of a talent of mine. I can immediately tell if a person prefers tea or coffee, and if they prefer coffee I can even tell what kind they're in the mood for, just by looking at their face. Maybe it was all that time I'd once spent working on the cash register of a large franchise coffee shop when I'd first moved to the city, watching customers' faces all day every day until I reached a point where I could predict their orders with incredible 95% accuracy.

Kuma seemed pleased with the coffee, drinking every last drop. He thanked me many times, stuffed a matsutake mushroom into my apron pocket by way of a thank you, then slowly strode off home along the mountain path that was bathed in the evening light.

I reached into my pocket and took out the mushroom. It was a high-quality one with its cap not yet opened. He must have gone high into the mountains that morning to pick it. It had such a wonderful aroma that I had to enjoy it right away. So I cooked part of it with some rice and steamed the other part in an earthen pot.

With all the windows fogged up in the kitchen, I hadn't even realized that the rains had finally stopped, leaving a beautiful sunset painted across the sky. It was a golden light that made it seem as if the world had been placed into a gigantic honey jar. And in my hands was an empty plate of pomegranate curry.

The next morning, at ten o'clock, a miracle happened in the form of Siñorita returning from the city with her daughter. Kuma had come by later to tell me all about it, describing how he'd been so excited that he'd accidentally put a different boot on each foot. But as I listened to his story a little more, things weren't as bright as they first appeared. It turned out that Siñorita had only returned to collect some things she'd left behind. Then she'd left again once she'd gathered them up, not even staying long enough for a cup of tea. But this didn't dampen Kuma's enthusiasm.

"Surely she wouldn't have come back unless she still had feelings for me," he said.

I didn't want to dampen his hopes. So I just listened and nodded.

Kuma was convinced that the pomegranate curry had changed his luck. I told him it was just a coincidence, but he kept going on about how special it had tasted and thanking me profusely with tears in his eyes. Then he shook my hand for a really long time with a grip that nearly crushed my bones, before setting off home again with a distinct spring in his step. My curry certainly didn't have the special powers he thought it did, but I was delighted to see how much he'd enjoyed it.

Inspired by his "miraculous" culinary experience, Kuma brought the lady who lived next door to him along to The Snail. She was known around town as the Mistress, though she wasn't actually Kuma's mistress. I'd known of her ever since I was a child, but since she was always dressed in her black mourning outfit all year round, I was a little scared to speak to her. She had once been the mistress of one of the most powerful men in the area. But the man had died during one of his visits to her house. Soon enough, the man's wife came by to claim the body and the Mistress was left all alone. There was talk that she'd spent the next three days and nights rolling around and laughing hysterically. But this was just a drunken rumour I'd overheard one time in Bar Amour, and though I didn't have much experience with this sort of thing, I couldn't help but feel that what might have sounded like laughter may just have been her way of expressing pain.

From the time her lover died, the Mistress underwent a complete change of personality. She even looked different – seeming to age by years over the period of mere weeks, taking on a sullen appearance, and wearing only mourning outfits day in and day out. Before all that had happened, the Mistress had a very outgoing personality. She also apparently looked after Kuma as a child as if he were the son she'd never had. So it was understandable why Kuma might want to bring her to The Snail to say thank you. And since the chandelier had been a gift from her to me, I felt it only right for me to do something for her too.

On the day of her meal, the Mistress came dressed in black from head to toe as always. Her legs seemed to be giving her some trouble, causing her to take very slow and careful steps as she supported her weight with her cane, and I was a little worried in case she might trip and fall. She also seemed to keep her head down as she walked, so I couldn't read the expression on her face. So she seemed like the same black figure I'd known of from years ago, like a ghost from the past; like a shadow of her former outgoing self.

The Mistress had visited The Snail with Kuma a few days earlier so we could all sit down and talk. But she'd turned out to be about as talkative as me, keeping her mouth shut the entire time. For a while, we tried communicating by writing on a piece of paper, but that didn't work too well either. So in the end I decided I'd have to create the menu all by myself.

At first I thought of selecting the best local ingredients to create something that was kind to the body – like fried shiitake mushrooms, sesame tofu, root-vegetable soup or steamed-egg pudding. These were exactly the kind of things my grandmother had taught me to make. But after thinking about it a little more, I decided to scrap the idea and start again. Then I came up with another notion – a meal designed to express the full range of human emotion, from delight to sorrow and from anger to pleasure. It would be a stimulating dinner encompassing an array of flavours, with desserts being soft and sweet, and spicy dishes bursting with heat. A dinner of flavours I imagined she'd never tasted before. A dinner with the power to bring the dying cells of her body back to life.

This is what I came up with.

Actinidia liquor cocktail
Bran-pickled apples
Oysters and sweet red sea bream carpaccio
Sangetan soup with a whole chicken brewed in shochu
Botargo risotto with freshly harvested rice
Lamb roast with wild mushroom garlic sauté
Yuzu sorbet
Mascarpone cheese tiramisu with vanilla ice cream
Dark espresso coffee

It may not have been a menu that would suit her elderly palate, and it may have made too much use of dairy products, too. But at the risk of sounding presumptuous, I wanted to show her that that the world was filled with delights she'd never known about before and to open the eyes of her soul that had been closed for far too long.

I spent several days in preparation, telling myself that I could always eat it if it turned out she didn't like it. I began by getting Kuma to drive me to the fish market at the crack of dawn to select the oysters and sweet red sea bream I'd be serving as an appetizer. Then I stuffed and spiced the chicken and left it marinating in a pot of soup and whipped up a tiramisu from milk, cream and mascarpone – all taken from the teat of the same cow.

When the Mistress had finally taken her seat, I handed her a blanket to place across her knees and showed her one of my messages.

Please wait a moment while I apply the finishing touches.

Then I poured an aperitif of white wine and actinidia liquor into a beautiful Baccarat glass before her. The actinidia, which had been aged for seven years, had been given to me by Kuma and was made from the seeds of the actinidia tree once the bugs had eaten the fruit. It was delicious on its own, but I felt the addition of a little white wine gave it some welcome depth and chose a variety from a local vineyard that had a fresh fruitiness that complemented the strength of the actinidia while giving the drink a deep, glistening yellow tone like liquid gold.

I glanced again at the glass, seeing the light of the chandelier reflected off it like a kaleidoscope, then I glanced out of the window to see Kuma give me a wave before getting back into his little truck for the drive home.

To whet her appetite, I started by giving the Mistress a slice of pickled apple. I'd made it by cutting an apple in half while leaving the skin intact, then salting it and leaving it in the bran vase for a couple of days. There was also a trick to giving them a milder flavour by letting them rest in the open air a little before serving, like leaving a good wine to breathe. With the plate set down in front of her, I gave a polite bow like a ballerina at a curtain call, then I wished her bon appétit and went quietly back to the kitchen. Then I put the copper pot of *sangetan* soup on the stove and cooked the chicken very slowly until it was done all the way to the core. Seeing it floating in its beautiful golden-brown soup, I thought back to when the chicken had been slaughtered just several days back, with the butcher twisting its neck, pulling down on its legs, plucking the feathers from its throat and then slicing an artery with a sharp knife, leaving the chicken flapping its wings as blood dribbled down its body. As a person who felt faint at the sight of a nosebleed or even my own menstrual blood, I desperately wanted to look away. But instead I forced myself to watch without blinking until the chicken eventually stopped moving. I'd caused a life to be taken for the sake of my dish. Now I saw it as my duty to do the best, for the chicken as well as the Mistress.

I'd taken special care to salt the chicken perfectly, adding just a pinch at a time until the flavour was just as I wanted. I was using a Hawaiian rock salt from near Diamond Head on the island of Oahu, with ginger and other herbs mixed in to create a sensation of coarse graininess tinged with a fantastic sweetness. I'd remembered how Kuma had told me about a photo of the Mistress and her man at a cottage somewhere in Hawaii and that's what had given me the idea.

I turned to take a peek through the curtains and back into the dining room. Just as I'd expected, the Mistress had touched neither her aperitif nor her appetizer yet. So I decided to wait a little longer before serving the *sangetan* soup. Outside, the light had already faded and I could hear a bird with a high-pitched call that seemed to be cheering me on. So I opened the window to hear better and saw a little feathered figure fly off toward the crescent moon and the solitary star shining next to it – like an embodiment of the Turkish flag that had hung in the restaurant I once worked in.

Hearing the jangling sound of cutlery, I took another peek back into the dining room where the Mistress was holding her knife and fork ready to set about the pickled apple. I was also happy to see that she'd sipped a little of her aperitif, too. So I quickly set about preparing the oysters and sweet-red-sea-bream carpaccio — slipping on a pair of work gloves to shuck open the juicy oysters, then placing them on a plain white plate alongside the sweet-red-sea-bream carpaccio, which I'd wrapped in seaweed for the afternoon along with a sprinkling of salt and a dash of olive oil. Then, after serving the carpaccio, I began on the *sangetan* soup — lifting the chicken out of its broth, quartering it with a large knife and setting free a plume of steam scented with burdock and sticky rice.

By the time I brought out the steaming *sangetan* soup, the Mistress had got through most of her aperitif and completely finished the pickled apple and raw oysters, leaving only a few slices of carpaccio on the plate. So I pushed the plate to the side, obeying my own house rule of never taking a plate away unless requested to by the customer, and put down the bowl of soup with its lid still in place. Then I bowed again like a ballerina and headed back once more to the kitchen.

Again, the Mistress took her time, eventually finishing everything, including the botargo risotto made with freshly harvested rice. And in the meantime, I put the finishing touches to today's main dish of roasted lamb. I'd begun by smothering the lamb with a generous coating of mustard before rolling it in a tray of breadcrumbs mixed with finely chopped garlic and rocket leaves. Some of the

75

things I like about lamb are its low cooking temperature and pleasant aftertaste which delicately dissipates after swallowing each morsel. I'd decided to accompany the lamb with mushrooms from a secret spot in the forest shown to me by Kuma just several hours earlier. In fact, it was a spot so secret that even his own relatives didn't know about it, so I felt happy to know how much trust he placed in me.

As I roasted the lamb in a frying pan, I stole another glance at the dining table and saw that the glass of aperitif was empty. So I took a moment's break from cooking to open a bottle of red wine and poured it into the Mistress's glass. It was a wine made from local grapes at the same vineyard as the white wine I'd served earlier, and it had a bold flavour and wonderful aroma that was a perfect match for the lamb.

After a while, I started to feel that her appetite may well be bigger than that of my old boyfriend and I wondered where, in that thin body of hers, she was managing to store it all. Then, just before Grandpa Owl was due to give his midnight call, the Mistress drank what remained of the bottle of wine and started on the yuzu sorbet I'd intended as a refreshing way to cleanse the palate. But despite her enjoying the wine, she gave no sign of being in the least bit inebriated. Instead, she remained the perfect lady right up to the end.

Leaving a glass of grappa to keep her company, I stepped out into the night air with the ingredients for the ice cream tucked under my arm. It was so cold out there that a chill ran right through to my bones, which was what made the outdoors such a perfect place for me to prepare the ice cream. Quickly, I poured iced water into a stainless steel bowl to make a chilled bain-marie. Then I beat all the ingredients together with a whisk with all the strength I could muster. I was out in the midst of nature with my ingredients before me, the stars shimmering above and my very own restaurant just steps away. And I was happier than I'd ever been before.

As I continued to beat out a steady rhythm, I added a dash of rum to the mix, drank in its delicious scent, then breathed it out as a foggy spirit to climb into the night sky. Then I turned back to face the eatery. On the material of the curtain, I could see the silhouette of the Mistress as she tipped back her shot of grappa. It was in a glass from the Taisho era that my grandmother had given to my mum, and it sparkled like a jewel in the Mistress's wrinkled hands.

I waited for the right moment, then I carried the ti-ramisu and vanilla ice cream to the table, along with a strong espresso made from Okinawan coffee beans. The Mistress closed her eyes and clasped her hands together, like a nun praying with all her heart.

I went back to the kitchen and watched the Mistress, as I'd watched Kuma the other day, with my hand mirror. Suddenly the gravity of her having lived more than seventy years hit me and I felt like I was watching some old foreign film from before the days of colour. I wondered how it must feel to go through every day mourning the loss of a loved one, always remembering, never smiling. Living a life of despair with an unfulfilled longing to see that one person you loved with all your heart.

I watched her bring the espresso to her thin lips and take a sip before taking a delicate scoop of the ice cream to her mouth. In the hand mirror, I saw her eyes close and I worried for a moment that the dessert might be too cold for her teeth. Then her eyes opened again and her face turned to the chandelier, her eyes set in a distant gaze. I wondered if its tiny lights brought to mind the light and warmth of the days spent in the arms of her lover. Then she took another sip of espresso, lifted a delicate spoon of tiramisu to her mouth, closed her eyes for another brief moment and turned her gaze back to the sparkle of the chandelier.

Moments later, the Mistress had finished every single item on my specially prepared menu. And in my hand mirror I saw her whisper in a voice as gentle as springtime sunshine, "*Gochisosama deshita*. That was delicious. Thank you very much."

She then bowed a deep and sincere bow.

This was the first time I'd ever heard her voice and I found it sensual, refined and smooth. It was a voice that momentarily mesmerized me, as if I'd been given a glimpse of her colourful youth. Then she stood up and said she'd like to lie down for a while. So I led her by the hand to my sofa bed of wine crates and felt the warmth of her fingertips against mine before she fell into a peaceful sleep that lasted until morning.

Several days later, the Mistress experienced a miracle of her own. For the first time in many years, she decided against wearing her mourning outfit and shunned the use of her cane, stepping out instead wearing ordinary, everyday clothing.

I'd been shopping for some daily items at the Yorozuya supermarket when I'd suddenly sensed a colourful presence behind me. And when I turned around, I was met with the sight of an elderly woman in the brightest of red coats, a hat with a fine plume of feathers and lipstick the shade of peaches. At first, I didn't even recognize her as the Mistress, thinking instead that some elderly woman from abroad must have happened across our village on her travels. Then I slowly recognized the face of the woman who'd enjoyed my meal just nights before.

I later heard from Kuma that she'd had dreamt of her lost lover while sleeping on the wine-crate sofa bed.

Apparently, she'd been praying every night for just a glimpse of him in her dreams, but it had never, ever happened. Not until that night at The Snail, when he'd appeared by her side and told her to enjoy her life because soon enough they would be together again for ever. According to Kuma, she looked happier than he'd ever seen her before. And she believed it was all because of my miraculous food. This is how the rumour began that swept through the village – that a meal at The Snail could fuel magic and provide the sustenance to make dreams come true.

On hearing the rumour about the Mistress, Momo – a young girl from the village – sent me a letter via Kuma. Not a text or an email, but a letter.

"I like Satoru." It said, "Can you get him to like me back?"

Momo had visited me several days earlier and told me all about her family, her school and her friends in a bright and cheerful manner. But when she came again with her friend Satoru, she'd been as quiet as a mouse. In fact they both had. Even after I'd shown them to their seats, they still said nothing and their shyness made me smile.

So I left them to their silence and returned to the kitchen to finish preparing the soup as the light from the window danced silently across the table, catching particles of dust in the air with a gentle caress. I'd really wanted to help Momo win Satoru's heart and had given some serious thought to what would be on the menu. At first, I thought it might be good to have something sweet and apple pie had come to mind, as had a Baumkuchen and crêpes. Then I imagined myself sitting there eating such desserts in front of my boyfriend and thought how such a dish requiring the skilful use of a knife and fork might prove to be stressful or embarrassing for a first date. So I decided to go with soup instead, which would go down smoothly even if they were both nervous or their hearts were burning with sweet-and-sour feelings. But I held off for a while before deciding on the ingredients, wishing to observe them together a little first.

Eventually, I selected a handful of vegetables, chopped them into small pieces and fried them in butter, beginning with the ones that would take the longest to cook. I chose the pumpkin because Satoru was wearing a bright mustard-coloured scarf which I thought was pretty. I chose carrots because I wanted to portray the sunset we could see spreading across the sky outside the window. And I selected apples because Momo's cute red cheeks made me think of them.

All these different images came together as one in the pot and I felt like an artist, instinctively choosing the paints for my palette – listening only to my intuition to create a unique dish on the spot. I boiled the sautéed vegetables in stock with a couple of bay leaves. Then I added a couple of other touches to make it more colourful, more creamy. And because love is strong enough on its own, I kept additional flavouring to a minimum, adding only a pinch of salt. Then I poured the soup into a red heart-shaped pot and quickly carried it to the table I'd set while the soup was simmering. I tried to move swiftly so they could enjoy the soup before it cooled. And as soon as I opened the lid, a warm steam floated up into the air like fairies on a mission to make this love happen. I noticed both of them watching my hands intently while I carefully poured the soup into wooden bowls. Then I placed wooden spoons on small place mats made of felt.

Bon appétit.

As always, I gave a deep bow before returning to the kitchen.

Once it had become dark outside, I brought some beeswax candles to the table and noticed that Satoru had changed seats to sit closer to Momo. I lifted the lid of the pot with a pounding heart and to my delight there was not even a spoonful left.

"Thank you," whispered Momo, with something in her voice that conveyed how much she might have wanted to freeze this moment in time – with the two of them huddled together, sharing their body heat like a couple of birds perched on a single branch. Doing my best not to disturb them, I wrote them a small note.

Are you warm enough?

But before they could respond, I noticed they were holding hands underneath the table. To think I'd played a part in making their love come to fruition was like lighting a little beeswax candle in my heart and I wanted to make myself scarce and leave them to it. So I left the empty wooden bowls, the spoons and the heart-shaped pot right where they were and returned to the kitchen. Then I purposely started making a noise in the kitchen, running the tap and cleaning my tools with gusto to give them the privacy they needed.

After I finished cleaning up in the kitchen, I thought of serving bite-size macaroons on the house to celebrate the birth of this new couple. I chose dark-pink macaroons with raspberry filling, placing them on a small plate and smiling to myself at the thought of how they might add even more sweetness to the evening. Half-skipping, I went to serve them, but managed to stop myself in the nick of time before coming through the curtain, having caught a glimpse of them sharing a soup-flavoured kiss. They were frozen in place, facing each other with their eyes closed, and although I wanted to watch them for ever, I felt it only appropriate to close the curtain again. Then I tiptoed out the back door and concentrated on pulling weeds from the herb garden for a while as the shimmering stars above seemed to sparkle in celebration of the lovers inside.

A part of me felt like sending the lovers home since it was already dark. But instead, I decided to let them stay as long as they wanted so they could make the most of every sweet second together. Then finally, as the full moon poked its face out from between the Twin Peaks, the two got up and left without letting go of each other's hands for even a second.

After that evening, the seasonal vegetable soup became a signature dish of The Snail. Someone even wrote about it on their blog, giving it the name "*je t'aime* soup". So after that, whenever customers came with dreams of realizing their love, that was what I served. But I used different combinations and proportions of vegetables each time, so I was often surprised by the way they turned out. These experiences changed my attitude towards vegetables immensely. Until then, I'd always thought I was the one making the food. But now I realized I was merely combining the flavours of foods that already existed. Perhaps it was the farmers who could be said to be creating the food. But then, although they could grow them, they could never make the seeds that gave them life. So the *je t'aime* soup taught me something very important, as well as filling the stomachs of many new couples who found their way to The Snail.

As a result of my matchmaking successes, I was asked to prepare a dinner with the same purpose at The Snail. It turned out that one of the regulars at Bar Amour was quite a skilled matchmaker herself and she'd begged my mum to set something up for two people she knew after hearing about my Je t'aime Soup. Both parties were in their late thirties and the matchmaker really wanted the dinner to be a success. I was against bringing two people together when they weren't interested in meeting, but if it was a case of helping two people who liked each other but didn't know how to take the first step, I was happy to help.

According to the matchmaker, the two people in question had been on a number of matchmaking dinners in the past. But since they both had rather high standards, none of those meetings had ever amounted to anything. The man was the heir to his father's farm, and though he presently worked for the local government in a neighbouring town, he did help out on the farm at weekends. But his parents were getting older and the day couldn't be far away when he'd be called upon to manage the farm by himself. The matchmaker also told me that the man was exceptionally shy, while the woman was a Japanese-language high-school teacher who was slender and pretty. As for height, the man was 168 cm tall, which meant he was noticeably shorter than the woman, who stood at 175 cm. But apparently this mismatch in height didn't bother them, with them both getting a good first impression from the initial photos they'd seen of each other. There did appear to be one problem, though. They apparently had completely different tastes in food. The man liked western cooking with heavy meat or a fish dish for the main course, while the woman sounded pretty close to being a vegetarian. Surely it would be impossible to create a menu that would please them both. Or even if I did, I worried there was a danger that the relationship might end up in divorce due to irreconcilable differences in diet.

"I don't care what kind of trick you pull," said the matchmaker, slapping my back. "I'm counting on you Ringo!"

On the day of their meal, the man and woman came to the matchmaker's house for formal introductions. Then, at just after lunchtime, they made their way to The Snail. The matchmaker was wearing a pink dress as if to stand out as the leader of the afternoon's events. Behind her, the man and woman walked in rather sheepishly. Then, after quite a long speech, the matchmaker said, "Well, that's enough of me talking. It's time for you to have your own conversation."

Then she winked at me and left.

Once the matchmaker's red Porsche had zoomed off, all three of us let out a big sigh of relief. I immediately went back into the kitchen and started preparing the meal. But

I couldn't help noticing that there was almost no conversation coming from the dining room.

After spending a long time working out how to please their differences in taste, I'd come up with a solution – a French course made with only vegetables. You see, most people seem to think you can't have a French course without meat or fish. But if you used vegetables that were really fresh and flavourful, there were tricks that could allow you to pull it off.

Drawing on my training at a French restaurant, I made one dish after the other, striving to maintain the delicate flavours, while giving the dish a bold and beautiful appearance. For the appetizer, I made a strawberry salad by marinating fresh rocket leaves, watercress and strawberries in boiled balsamic vinegar. Then for my first main dish, I made fried carrots – cutting the carrots in half vertically while leaving the skin intact, then breading them and frying them lightly in vegetable oil. When the carrots were ready, I placed them on top of the salad and was happy to see how closely they resembled deep-fried shrimp.

For the next main dish, I prepared a steak of Japanese radish. I sautéed lightly boiled radish together with half-dried shiitake mushrooms. Then I used salt, soy sauce and olive oil for seasoning. For drinks, both the man and woman had begun by requesting only water.

But by halfway through, they changed their minds – ordering one glass of red wine and one glass of white. By this time, there was still no conversation in the air. But I could tell from their expressions that they were enjoying themselves.

For a third dish, I made a risotto, although it wasn't technically French. I added puréed spinach, wheat and crushed walnuts to give it more volume and I also added some dried tomato and parsley. Then, for the day's Je t'aime Soup, I combined all the vegetables I had in the kitchen – onions, leeks, potatoes, spinach, pumpkin, carrots, sweet potatoes, paprika, burdock, lotus root, Japanese radish, Chinese cabbage, cauliflower and more. I even added a handful of clover I'd taken from the banks of the canal and threw in the peel of the radishes and carrots I'd used to make the main courses.

As I took my first sip of the soup, I nearly passed out! It was so good already that it didn't even need any salt! Those fresh vegetables had already provided all the flavour I'd hoped for. I waited until I'd got the purple potato crème brulée baking away in the oven, then I stepped into the dining room with my heart pounding and took a memo out from my apron pocket.

How is everything?

I held the memo in front of me so both of them could see it clearly.

"I've never had such a wonderful meal of vegetable dishes!" said the teacher first.

"It was fantastic. Were the vegetables specially delivered from somewhere?" said the man immediately after her.

I'd been hoping they'd ask that, so I nearly jumped for joy when they actually did. I quickly tried to jot down a message on the memo pad, but my fingers wouldn't work fast enough to convey the excitement I felt in my heart. So I gave up and decided to use my hand and body gestures to explain that all the vegetables had actually been grown on the farm owned by the man's family!

"What?" he exclaimed, with a look of total surprise and the woman seemed surprised too.

I'd asked Kuma to take me to the man's farm a few days earlier to get all the vegetables I needed. But I hadn't said a word to anyone else. According to the matchmaker, the heir to the farm wasn't thrilled at the prospect of running his own farm. So I'd wondered if by preparing such a meal, I might be able to help change his mind. To me, this would be a more important outcome than the success of their date.

Just then, the oven timer rang out and I rushed back into the kitchen to sprinkle unrefined sugar on the crème brulée before using a small blowtorch to make the characteristic solid surface. Then I served it quickly and with a pot of rose tea, making sure it was still piping hot by the time they started on it. Then, at long last, their conversation began.

A little while later, the matchmaker came to pick the two of them up. I was overjoyed to have brought them a little closer together and I felt I'd played a part in adding a gentle warmth to each of their lives, like the flamingo pink of the sunset sky above us.

Unfortunately, not everyone in the village welcomed me with open arms. One day I was paid a surprise visit by several officers from the Department of Sanitary Control. Apparently someone had told them some nonsense, saying that I was mixing roasted newt into my dishes! According to the oldest officer, there was an old wives' tale that said you could make a very effective love potion by roasting a male and a female newt, then grinding them into a powder together. You could then sprinkle the powder onto an unsuspecting person's food or even mix it into their drink, apparently.

Well this was the first I'd ever heard of anything like that! I did enjoy watching little newts as they flapped their little arms, legs and tails in the water. But I'd never once considered roasting the cute little things! Luckily, the officers seemed to believe me. Nevertheless, they went around the place having a look in the drawers and cupboards before they signed off the case.

Since it was lunchtime anyway, the officers each had a *wai-wai* bowl before heading out, which is a dish of Neapolitan spaghetti on rice. It was a dish my grandmother invented and she often served it whenever she needed to fix a quick meal, which was pretty often considering how nice she was in serving all kinds of guests to her house, including the door-to-door salespeople who'd come to sell medicines and even the telephone engineer who'd come to fix our line.

Though the roasted newt incident turned out to be quite laughable, there was a more serious incident a few days later that was no laughing matter at all. Kuma had introduced me to one of his friends' friends via email. I usually try to meet my guests beforehand to discuss the menu, but this guy kept claiming to be too busy, so we'd just exchanged several emails instead. But they were always very short emails that didn't really give me the information I needed and I was getting the impression that he might be the sort of person who finds it rather hard to talk about himself.

Since he was only available between three and four in the afternoon, I decided to make an exception and have two customers in one day, letting him in before the reservation for dinner. By the end of our email exchanges, I'd only learnt that his budget was just a thousand yen and that he wanted to eat a sandwich. Considering that he was coming just two or three hours after lunch, I figured he might not be hungry enough to eat anything too heavy, so I decided I'd make him a fruit sandwich.

Pears were in season, so I took the Snail Mobile to visit the fruit farm at the edge of the village and chose a handful that were just on the cusp of ripening so they would be perfect for when I needed them. And after spending four to five days in the eatery kitchen, sure enough, they started releasing a soft, sweet smell.

On the day of the sandwich, I awoke so early that the air still carried the scent of night and started my preparations. I made a point of using organic flour for an English dough, mainly because I felt that Japanese flour had a different feel to it when kneading. I'd let some raisins soak in water overnight to make them soft, which I then added to the dough. Then I slammed the dough on the kitchen counter over and over again until it was firm, but with just the right texture before leaving it to rest and rise over several hours.

I prepared some cream by mixing single cream with heavy cream made by removing the milk serum from yogurt. Yogurt cream was made the same way as in the Indian desert known as shrikhand, which my boyfriend had made for me from time to time and I'd remembered how to hang the yogurt over the sink in a cloth to drain. So by morning, there was only a heavy cream left in there. Single cream on its own would have made my dish too rich, whereas the yogurt alone would have been too light. So by mixing the two, I felt I'd achieved just the right degree of richness, freshness and consistency to hold the fruit in place and prevent its juices from soaking the bread.

By lunchtime, the raisin bread had finished baking, so all that was left to do was to prepare the sandwich before the customer arrived. That also meant I had plenty of time to start work for my dinner reservation, which was for a table of nine – quite a lot of customers for The Snail! Again, the purpose of the dinner was to bring together two of those customers and I'd decided on making a big pot of bouillabaisse for everyone to enjoy together. And since Kuma had already delivered the fresh seafood, I was ready to go.

At two thirty, it was time to begin putting the sandwich together. So I put all the fish parts into a plastic bag and secured it in the bucket I used to make Hermes's food. Then I used toothpaste and baking soda, as well as soap, to wash my hands thoroughly so as not to transfer the fish smell to the sandwich.

I focused my thoughts on the raisin bread and began slicing it with a bread knife, my hands feeling cool from the effect of the toothpaste. Then I spread a thin layer of melted milk chocolate on the surface of the bread to prevent the bread from soaking up the juice and to give it more flavour. I'd chosen milk chocolate instead of dark chocolate because it went better with cream and fruit and I'd wanted to create an effect in which you would bite into

93

the sandwich, feel the juices of the fruit spreading across the soft bread, and then feel a hint of chocolate spreading through your mouth as you started to chew.

Feeling that the cream might need a little more flavour, I dribbled in a little honey from a neighbour that happened to keep bees. Then, right before it was time for my guest to arrive, I peeled the pears, cut them into thin slices and placed them between the pieces of bread covered with cream. I then cut the sandwich into bite-sized pieces and plated them. The white bread, the milk-white cream and the golden-white pears came together to create a breathtaking gradation and the raisins added a nice polka-dot accent too.

When my customer came to the door, I bowed deeply to welcome him before going back to the kitchen to finish preparing my dish. He turned out to be much older than I'd expected from our email exchange and his hair was about three-quarters grey. He was small in stature but with a good build and he was wearing a blue-and-white striped shirt with an expensive-looking navy vest and a port-coloured scarf around his neck. He actually seemed a lot nicer than I'd expected. It was always difficult to cook for someone for the first time and I'd been quite nervous until actually meeting him. But now he was here, I felt more relaxed and even able to guess which type of tea he'd like.

I decided on a souchong – a slightly spicy, tangy tea that would work well with the fresh flavours of the sandwich.

So even if he felt the cream of the sandwich was too much, the souchong would clear his palate. I let it steep for a minute or two, then I placed it on the table with his sandwich, gave my ballerina bow and returned quietly to the kitchen.

Everything about the sandwich had turned out just perfect – the baking of the bread, the softness of the raisins, the sweetness of the cream and the ripeness of the pears. In fact, it may have even been the best fruit sandwich I had ever made. My heart was so filled with expectations for it. But perhaps I'd been too hasty.

"What the hell is this?" an annoyed voice bellowed out, accompanied by the sound of a fist hitting the table and the rattling of cups and plates. I rushed out of the kitchen and ran to his side, still with no idea of what he was talking about. I wondered for a moment if it might be some sort of joke. But again, I was way off the mark.

"What on earth is this!" he said, holding up a strand of hair with a look of disgust. More specifically, it was a strand of pubic hair.

"In a sandwich of all places! This has to be the worst eatery I've ever been to!"

Then he kicked up at the table with the tip of his shoe, sending the lid of the sugar pot onto the table.

I couldn't believe my eyes! I'd always been so careful about preventing things from getting into my food.

95

Beneath the cloth on my head I was basically bald and this was certainly not one of those smutty no-panties cafés – I always wore underwear and slacks in the kitchen at all times! So I had absolutely no idea how that hair might have found its way into the food. Before I could say anything at all, the man stood up and left. But on his way out, he showed me the screen of his digital camera with a close-up image of my sandwich and the protruding hair. I was absolutely burning with rage. I'd used such wonderful fresh ingredients and I so hated the idea of letting them go to waste, even though they were sitting there looking rather disgusting with a solitary pubic hair placed on top. Recently, I'd been feeding Hermes with the leftovers from the eatery. But I felt it just wouldn't be right to do that with the fruit sandwich and tossed it all into the rubbish bin. I'd put so much effort into it that it would be like drowning my own child!

As I stood there considering the sandwich, a single tear trickled down my cheek and fell into the rubbish bin. I added a lot of milk and sugar to the now lukewarm souchong and downed it while standing up. After all, it was no fault of the souchong. I savoured its smoky aroma and felt myself becoming a little calmer. Then I took a deep breath and felt the anger subside a little more. There were all sorts of people in this world. I understood this in my mind, but my heart just wasn't getting it. I learnt later on from Kuma that the man was running an old bakery at the edge of the village, but he'd been losing a lot of custom recently. Perhaps that was connected to the way he'd reacted that day.

Living in the days of the Internet, I expected that digital image to surface sooner or later on a site somewhere and put an end to The Snail. But after a week, then a month had passed, I still hadn't seen or heard anything about it. In fact, the only thing I kept hearing were apologies from Kuma, who felt so bad about introducing a man he hardly knew himself in the first place.

"Ringo," he kept saying. "I'm so sorry you had to go through that."

Ever since that reservation, both Kuma and I were more cautious about the reservations I would accept. And although I was still sure the incident had not been my fault, I took even more precautions against foreign objects falling into my food and I tried to make myself feel better by imagining that the god of cooking had merely sent a sign to tell me not to get too big-headed now that things at The Snail were going really well.

In late November, a girl with her hair in a bob came running into The Snail. I remember the day clearly because the tips of the Twin Peaks were covered in snow, making it look as if they were wearing some gigantic lacy bra. It was late in the afternoon and the weather outside was cloudy. It seemed as if it was going to rain, so I was happy to be indoors, preparing hamburger steaks for a family party of six that night.

When the girl burst in, she looked terribly desperate and, just like the weather outside, she seemed ready to start raining tears at any moment.

"Please help me!" she said.

My hands were covered in minced meat so I was unable to reach for my notebook. Then the girl dropped her school bag on the floor, and very carefully took out a box from a paper bag she was holding. I noticed that her bright-red and rather beaten bag had an old *omamori* charm hanging from it, and on that charm was the name Kozue, written by the hand of an adult.

Supporting the bottom of the box gently, she made her way over to the table and placed it down with great care. Then she slowly opened the lid to reveal a rabbit inside.

"She's weak!" said the girl. "Please, help her!"

I looked inside the box, feeling that this girl Kozue might be in greater need of help than the rabbit. Then I quickly washed my hands so I could make her something to drink. I hadn't lit the wood stove yet, so the eatery felt like the inside of a refrigerator and our breath turned white in the air. To take the chill off, I decided to prepare some hot cocoa. So using a small knife, I shaved thin pieces of milk chocolate into a porcelain pot, put the pot over a low flame, then gradually thinned it out by adding milk. All the while, Kozue remained hugging the box as it sat on her trembling knees. As I let the cocoa simmer for a while, I opened my notebook to a clean page and wrote in big, childish letters.

What happened?

When I thought the cocoa was ready, I topped it off with a generous amount of honey as well as a secret ingredient – a few drops of a sophisticated cognac. Then I gently placed some lightly whipped cream on the surface, like a floating cloud, then a fresh sprig of mint on the top. I knew that mint had a calming effect and I was hoping it would work its magic on Kozue.

I took the pot of freshly prepared cocoa over to the table where Kozue was sitting. Seeing that she was still quivering, I opened my notebook and showed it to her. Then, after splitting the cocoa in two café-au-lait bowls, I placed one in front of her and gestured for her to go ahead. Kozue hesitantly reached out for her bowl, with the rabbit box still on her knees. On her little nails were drawings of a rabbit with a coloured marker pen, and just for a fleeting moment I noticed her expression appear to relax a little as the warm steam from the cocoa rose to her face. Then, after taking a sip, she filled me in on the situation.

ITO OGAWA

She'd found the rabbit on the street on her way to
school about a week ago. It was in a bigger box then,
along with some hay and food. There had also been a
letter inside the box, presumably written by the previous owner, which Kozue took out from her pocket and
showed to me.

*Due to personal reasons, I can no longer take care of this
rabbit.*

Those were the only words printed on the sheet of paper.
So Kozue took the rabbit home. But unfortunately, her
mother wasn't fond of animals and wouldn't allow her
to keep it. She had told Kozue to take the rabbit back to
where she'd found it. But there was no way Kozue could
bring herself to abandon such a poor, defenceless animal.
Without telling her mother, she had been looking after
it, keeping it in the wardrobe of her room at night, and
taking it to school during the day. However, the rabbit had
gradually stopped eating the food Kozue fed her, and for
a couple days it hadn't eaten a thing.

I picked up the box holding the anorexic rabbit and
examined it carefully. I could make out the faint scent
of grass from near its nose and it had beautiful silver-
grey hair, like a kitchen sink that had been painstakingly
scrubbed. The inside of its ears were a soft salmon pink

and its pitch-black eyes were glossy, like the surface of coffee jelly. This rabbit had clearly led a good life – or at least used to.

Will you let me look after her for just one day?

I wrote in my notebook before handing it to Kozue. Then she bit her bright-red lips and gave a big, enthusiastic nod. I hoped that my actions might restore her faith in adults. But what if I couldn't help? Would she spend the rest of her life hating me or unable to believe anything adults said?

As Kozue took a deep breath, picked up her bag and left, I realized I only had twenty-four hours to produce results and the clock was ticking. Fair enough, this was The Snail, a place of miracles. But could I have any success with an anorexic rabbit? It took a lot of counselling to help a person through the same disorder, after all, so what chance could I have with an animal that couldn't even understand me?

So as not to startle the rabbit, I blew onto my hands to warm my fingertips, then cautiously touched its back. I could feel the outline of its spine. It really was a thin rabbit. There was no strength in its ears, and even its whiskers seemed to be lacking spirit. The rabbit's expression remained blank, even when I held its round tail between my fingers. I didn't think I would get a reaction out of it even if I tickled it!

Carefully, I slid the palms of my hands under the rabbit's stomach and picked it up in both hands. I could feel its heart against the palms of my hand, and if I closed my eyes I could imagine I was holding nothing more than that throbbing life. But despite the beating heart, the rabbit's body was limp and stretched out like a piece of *mochi*.

I placed my face in front of the rabbit's and looked into its eyes. But its gaze wouldn't settle, and it was impossible to tell where it was looking. Its dark coffee eyes seemed to be staring far into the past, deep down an old, dark, bottomless well, and I started to feel a little unsettled as I stared into them.

This rabbit is suffering from apathy, loneliness and utter despair.

That would have been my diagnosis if I were an animal psychologist.

I gave up trying to get a reaction out of the rabbit and gently placed it back in the box.

Tonight's guests were a family that ran a laundry service out by the hot springs. The reservation had been made by the mother for a dinner celebrating the birthday of the grandfather who lived with them and the request had been for the entire family of six to be served a children's meal.

"Dear Grandpa isn't really all there any more," explained the mother in a grave voice when she'd visited The Snail a few days earlier.

The green-tea-and-sweet-bean chiffon cake I'd baked the night before was now in the freezer. I'd prepared eight thick candles and five thinner ones to go on top of the cake since there was simply no space to place as many candles as he had years. All I had left to do now was to fry the chicken rice and hamburger steaks when the timing was right and wait for the party to arrive.

Using the time I had to spare, I took some of the extra carrot glacé I'd made earlier, mashed it with a fork and set it aside for the rabbit on a small plate. I had the carrots regularly delivered by the farmer's son who'd come to the eatery with the teacher and they were absolutely amazing, with a hint of sweetness that lingered and a firmness that seemed to withstand even boiling for a prolonged period of time. Then I brought out one of the wine crates left over from when I was making the sofa bed and placed some scrunched-up newspapers inside it, along with the plate of mashed carrots and a little bowl of water. I then moved the box to the corner and went to fetch the rabbit. As I lifted the rabbit again, I realized how it felt a little like freshly pounded *mochi*. It seemed heavy and weary, as if it had lost all will to live.

After placing the rabbit in its new home, I knelt down and tried to carry a teaspoon of carrot glacé to its mouth. But the rabbit didn't respond. So I turned my attention to trying to get some water in its mouth instead. But again, the rabbit just stared into the distance with emotionless eyes. Then I suddenly got the idea of taking the carrot leaf and tickling the rabbit's nose with it. But still it didn't respond. Perhaps it really did have some sort of eating disorder.

Soon it was time to continue preparing for the children's meal. So I did my best to put all thoughts of the rabbit aside for a moment and concentrate on the task at hand. After all, I wouldn't be much of a professional if I let a single weary rabbit get in the way of my preparations.

Using all the burners on the stove, I carefully cooked the hamburger steaks, the chicken rice, the fried shrimp and the sautéed pumpkins all at once. Then I brought out the large plates from the cabinet, gave them a wipe-over with a towel and placed them on the table. I then served up the four different foods of the dish on the six plates in front of me, thinking how I'd made so many different dishes in my life yet never put so much effort into a children's meal. When I'd finished, the dishes were both colourful and well balanced, with a mix of vegetables, meat and seafood. I'd also kept the portions relatively small since the mother had told me they were not big eaters, but there was still plenty to satisfy an adult appetite. All in all, it was looking very good and I wanted to give myself an A grade for both content and presentation.

For a little while, I couldn't decide whether to stick a flag in the mounds of chicken rice that sat at the centre of

THE RESTAURANT OF LOVE REGAINED

each plate. Then, with only fifteen minutes left, I decided a flag would be good after all, so I set about hastily making them out of tiny rectangles of paper and toothpicks before drawing a little yellow snail on each in crayon. Within moments of completing my last flag, the family drove up outside, with the mother at the wheel.

To my surprise, there was no one in the family that you could really call a "kid". The oldest brother was a uniformed high-schooler with an adult face, and though the younger sister dressed in the sweats of a local junior high had some childish features, she was still clearly past the age of wanting a children's meal. Then came the grandpa, who was pushing the grandmother along in a wheelchair, while wearing a steely expression.

Almost as soon as the family had sat down, I started to get the impression that the grandpa wasn't exactly "not really all there" as the mother had led me to believe. In fact, he wasn't there at all! But I could understand why she wouldn't want to mention that. What's more, I began to understand the request for the children's meal, which wasn't for the sake of the school kids but for the grandpa himself.

As soon as the kid's meal was placed in front of the grandpa, he began stuffing his mouth with food. But he didn't use the spoon or fork or chopsticks. Instead he just used his hands. From time to time, he'd start mumbling, as if chanting some sort of spell with food still stuffed in his mouth. But the words made no sense to me and it seemed they meant nothing to his family either.

One particularly unusual thing that became apparent was that the grandpa seemed to be labouring under the impression that the woman in the wheelchair was not his wife, but actually his mother. He also seemed to be treating his son and his son's wife as if they were total strangers, talking to the grandson as if he was his comrade from the war, and acting as if the granddaughter was his friend. He'd also break the silence occasionally with a sudden outburst of swearing, which would make the entire family blush. But not once did anyone ever get annoyed or raise their voice, no matter how bad the grandpa's manners became.

Since the portions were relatively small, the family of six finished their meal in no time. The mother had mentioned that they were in a bit of a hurry, so I quickly cleared the plates, changed the tablecloth and put out the birthday cake.

I went to darken the room, leaving the candles on the cake as the only illumination, and the family started to sing *Happy Birthday* together while clapping their hands. At first it was only the mother's slightly off-tune soprano voice that sounded a little teary, but eventually the daughter's voice turned teary as well, and then the son, followed by the father and finally, like a virus, the grandmother, until in the end, the room was filled with a chorus of teary voices.

After the song ended, they all shouted, "Congratulations, Grandpa!" Then – just as I was expecting them to give him a round of applause – they all burst into tears! It was almost as if he'd died and they were already grieving. As for Grandpa, his expression held its same steely look as he blew out the candles one by one with weak breaths. Then, just for a moment, The Snail was enveloped in a dark silence.

After I put the lights back on again, the silence continued as the family dug into the cake. I wondered what on earth had happened to this family. The grandpa had clearly gone a bit senile. But why did the entire family have tears running down their cheeks?

I got the answer when the family was getting up to leave and the mother walked over to pay. "We're going to take him to a nursing home now," she said, forcing a polite smile. "The six of us have lived as a family for all these years, so it's hard for us. But I'm very grateful for tonight. For some reason, Grandpa always falls asleep after he has a kid's meal. So we thought the best time to take him to a home would be right after a meal like this."

I looked out of the window to where Grandpa was pushing his wife's wheelchair along, never letting anyone else lend a hand.

"It's not like we won't see him again," said the mother as I gave her the change. "And we'll come here again. When we do, please can you make the children's meal again? Grandpa loves it and yours was so much tastier than anything I could ever make."

And with that, the mother headed back to the car, where all the family was now waiting, and I stepped outside as well to wave them off.

For just a moment, I caught a glimpse in the moonlight of the grandpa's face in the back window – with his mouth hanging open and his eyes staring blankly out into the corners of the universe. He looked to me like he knew the fate that awaited him. Then his face disappeared into the chilly late autumn night along with the van and I stepped back inside to where the rabbit was wearing the grandpa's steely expression.

The rabbit was lying sideways in the wooden crate with its legs and hands dangling, neither fully awake nor asleep.

Hey you, you're going to die if you go on like this, I said to the rabbit in my mind.

I checked the mark I'd left on the water bowl to see if the rabbit had drunk any. But it seemed the rabbit hadn't even taken a sip. There was, however, a glimmer of hope. Earlier on in the evening, when I'd taken Grandpa's cake from the fridge, I'd noticed the rabbit lift its head slightly and give it a glance. Unfortunately, I hadn't been able to cut off a small slice for the rabbit, but its reaction had given me a clue to its past and I let my imagination run free while baking the rabbit a biscuit instead.

Judging by its shiny coat, I imagined that the previous owner of the rabbit had treated it very well and that somewhere that owner still loved it. The typed letter had appeared kind of brusque, but I wondered if the owner might have kept its wording to a minimum as a way to stop his or her feelings from spilling over. The rabbit also seemed to be of a pedigree breed. Not that I knew that much about thoroughbred rabbits. But I could at least tell that it was much more regal-looking than any of the ones we'd ever kept while I was at school. So I started to wonder if maybe the rabbit had been the pet of a rich family and had at one time been showered with love and affection.

Now that my imagination was chugging along, I took the story further in my mind. I began to wonder if something had happened that was beyond the family's control; something that had forced them to give up the rabbit in spite of their deep feelings for it. Perhaps the grandmother who'd been taking care of the rabbit had passed away, or perhaps the family had had to move to an apartment that didn't allow pets. Perhaps the rabbit was just like the senile grandpa, with the family wanting to go on living together but there being some reason why that could no longer go on. I began to wonder if the grandpa had on some level understood the difficult decision his family had had to make, and if the rabbit might have somehow understood its situation too. After all, neither of them spoke, and both of them wore the same steely expression.

But even if they couldn't understand their situation, would that make the loneliness any less painful? How did the rabbit feel in that box in which it was abandoned? Seeing the pitch blackness. Hearing the approaching footsteps. Listening to the familiar voices growing distant. Feeling the total isolation.

Surely the rabbit must have been crying in the dark, yearning desperately to see its master again, to be held in its master's arms just one more time. Perhaps rabbits couldn't shed tears. But I bet they can cry on the inside. Perhaps this rabbit in my eatery was all cried out. With no hope left in its heart and nothing familiar to rest its eyes upon. Maybe this was why the rabbit had lost all interest in feeding.

As I used both hands to mix the ingredients for the biscuits – the vegetable oil, sugar, walnuts, wholewheat flour and water – I let my thoughts turn to the rabbit's hidden past. It was all pure speculation, of course, but I imagined that the rabbit had come from a wealthy family, where it had been fed sweets on a daily basis. Maybe that was why it had reacted the way it did to the sweet aroma of my chiffon cake. And maybe it was worth trying to tempt the rabbit with something sweet.

I rolled out the dough on the cooking board until it was flat and even, then I sprinkled dried lavender on top of it; lavender can help give you a lift when you're feeling down. Then I cut the dough into rabbit-bite-sized pieces and baked them in the oven at 200 degrees Celsius.

I couldn't help but keep thinking about the grandpa and I wondered if he'd reached the home already. If only he could remain in a deep and restful sleep, where he'd never have to experience the pain of parting from his family. Thinking about sleep made me realize how tired I was too. So I decided to spend the night at The Snail and started to lay out the futon on the sofa bed of wine crates on which the Mistress had dreamt of her departed lover.

I checked back on the biscuits and, seeing they were ready, I took them from the oven to let them cool. The dough for Hermes's bread was also ready for the morning. But my day had not ended yet. I wasn't about to let it end until the rabbit had taken some food. I simply couldn't let Kozue down. The look on her face when she'd entrusted me with the rabbit was burnt on my mind like the light of the first evening star and I was determined to take responsibility for nursing it back to health. So I gathered up the rabbit in my arms and got in under the futon covers.

111

The footsteps of winter were approaching and once the wood stove was off, the air in the eatery turned cold almost immediately. Fortunately, the futon was nice and warm. Though I wasn't naive enough to think I could win the rabbit's trust right away, I did imagine I might be able to give it the affection that it must have been missing. After all, if I was an abandoned rabbit, I'd want somebody to hold me too!

Lying down in the futon, I positioned myself to face the rabbit. Then I placed the freshly baked biscuits onto the palm of one hand and kept stroking the rabbit's body with the other. The scent of fresh lavender and sweet biscuits gradually filled the inside of the covers, and once I turned the lights off, only the rabbit's coffee jelly eyes reflected the outside.

I closed my eyes and continued to stroke the rabbit. That night I was to be the guardian of the rabbit's breathing. I kept waking up with a start, then anxiously holding my palm to the motionless rabbit's nose to make sure it was still breathing. And in that drowsy state, I'd also count the number of biscuits left on my palm. But unfortunately, not a single piece was gone.

I continued to drift lightly in the blurred limbo between slumber and wakefulness. It was as if I was constantly deep in thought – overwhelmed by the fear that the rabbit might die in its sleep and by my responsibility to my new friends, Kozue and the rabbit. I didn't want to disappoint my new human friend. And I didn't want my furry friend to die.

Eventually the sky outside started to brighten and I could hear the sounds of birds chirping. Feeling something strange on my hand, I opened my eyes to find the eatery enveloped in a bright and pure light – a light so bright that, for a moment, I was left blinded. I felt like I'd emerged from a far deeper sleep than usual and woken to find the world already bustling with life.

Just after waking, I felt a strange feeling on my palm – it was the rabbit licking away with its cute pink tongue. I pulled back the covers to see its ears and whiskers all perky, like a dried-up plant that's been watered back to life. But what I couldn't see was a single biscuit. For a moment, I looked around the bed, wondering if they'd simply fallen onto the floor. But they hadn't. There was no question about it; the rabbit had eaten all the biscuits, crumbs and all!

I gave the rabbit a warm embrace. Gentle so as not to hurt it, but firm enough to convey my love for it. Then I placed some more biscuits inside the wooden crate, put down a fresh bowl of water, placed the rabbit inside and watched the blue-and-red veins on the inside of its ears – like beautiful embroidery in the sunlight. I was proud of the fact that I'd kept my promise to Kozue. I was also incredibly relieved. Then I heard Hermes's cries coming from outside, prompting me to get up and prepare her breakfast.

That afternoon, at around the same time as the day before, Kozue came to The Snail – her expression as hard as an unripe plum. Then I showed her the recovered rabbit. In the hours since it had eaten the biscuits, the rabbit had perked up so much that it had begun to hop all around the inside of the eatery, until I'd eventually had to make a collar out of an old wristwatch and a length of string so it could hop around the herb garden as well. The rabbit didn't seem to mind, though. If anything, it seemed to like being tethered; as if it was a bond rather than a restraint.

Kozue picked up the rabbit very carefully and held it in her arms. She told me this was the first time she'd ever picked it up since she'd always been afraid of accidentally hurting it. I wondered if that might have contributed to the rabbit not eating too. As Kozue continued to play with the rabbit, I proceeded to prepare afternoon tea. A few days earlier, I'd gone out into the woods to pick up some chestnuts to make *marron glacé*, being careful to reserve some of the more misshapen ones for making "Mont Blanc" cakes. They were meant to be served as desserts for dinner guests, but I'd made a few extra in case of occasions like this and I was looking forward to pairing their creaminess with the lovely Earl Grey tea that was now steeping in the pot.

Though it was a little chilly outside, I set out a table and chairs in the garden and brought out some blankets to place over our knees as we enjoyed the afternoon tea – the rabbit, Kozue and me. I was happy to see Kozue pick up the rabbit again, place her on her lap and hold her tight. It was wonderful to see her laughing and smiling too, unlike the sad Kozue who'd visited only days ago.

It had been a physically exhausting twenty-four hours, but at the same time it had been very rewarding emotionally. I sat there resting while the rabbit gently nibbled some cake from Kozue's maple-leaf-like palm. At first, I worried a little about the butter and liquor I'd put in the cake. But the rabbit didn't seem to mind at all, and Kozue was chewing away happily too while wearing the same cute expression as the rabbit.

I'm so glad I started this eatery, I thought to myself while gazing at the beautiful misty-white Twin Peaks.

"My mother is going to let me keep the rabbit, so I'm going to look after it at home. Thank you so much!" said Kozue in a clear, determined voice, as if making a promise to the late-autumn sky. Somewhere behind her, a deer came out of the trees and gave a glance in our direction. Winter was just around the corner.

Sometimes magic can strike from out of the blue. When I opened the curtains one December morning, the view outside was a scene of the brightest white. It was as if rivers of milk had covered the land and as if meringue had fallen from the sky, and for some reason I imagined the pure white snowflakes landing on the Mistress's new vividly colourful coat.

My customers for Christmas were a gay couple who had eloped to the village. The two men were now on their secret honeymoon and I didn't want to disrupt the romantic atmosphere, so with the help of Kuma I decided to cater to the bungalow at the lake where the couple was spending the night. On the way back from delivering their meal, I felt kind of like Santa Claus as Kuma and I whizzed through the night on his snowmobile at great speed, cutting through the fluffy snowflakes that fell from the sky and enjoying a natural high, without the assistance of even a drop of alcohol.

Cooking is everything. It's all it takes to send a wave of joy throughout every cell of my being. And when I cook for someone else, that's all I need to feel true happiness from the bottom of my heart. *Thank you cookery. Thank you!* If I'd shouted those words a million times into the night sky, it wouldn't have been enough. I'd never be satisfied until those words reached every person in the world or until my inner voice gave out. That's how strongly I felt.

We parked the snowmobile for a few minutes on the way back and Kuma and I looked up into the night sky together while resting our arms on each other's shoulders. For the briefest of moments, the snowflakes seemed to stop and the myriad points of light sparkled in the infinite distance. It was all so magical that I felt like telling Kuma that he could give me a kiss. Just this once. If that was what he wanted.

I spent the end of the year cleaning the kitchen from corner to corner with baking powder. And although it was nothing elaborate, I was able to make a traditional New Year's *osechi* just in time for New Year's Eve. When my grandmother had been alive, we used to go all out and make an elaborate *osechi*. We'd fill layer upon layer of boxes with a variety of dishes until it began to resemble a cubist painting or some beautiful mosaic. Every year, I'd be mesmerized by it. We'd sit and slurp our *soba* noodles while watching the annual New Year's singing contest on TV, we'd exchange New Year greetings with toasts of spiced *toso* sake, and we'd spend the rest of the holidays washing the remaining *osechi* down with sake.

After my grandmother passed away and I started living with my boyfriend, we'd have a small Indian-style New Year's celebration of our own in the room we shared. The New Year's custom in India is to wear something brand-new. So for that special day, I'd wrap myself in a Punjabi suit, which is a loose-fitting one-piece dress made from thin silk and loose trousers that Indian girls wear before they get married. I'd complete the look with a long scarf around my neck. Then I'd make a traditional Indian fried pie out of cashews, coconuts and almonds. I'm sure it didn't taste anything like the ones he'd find back home, but I was happy just to be able to spend that special time with him.

Mum had jetted off to Hawaii with a few of her regular customers and she wasn't due back until several days later. So I was left to spend New Year's all by myself. Or with Hermes at least. It was a rather meagre New Year's celebration for me that year, with those beautiful layers of my grandmother's *osechi* replaced by *osechi* served in Tupperware.

I went outside and wished Hermes a Happy New Year, but of course she didn't respond. Occasionally, I'd find myself getting a little bored, so I'd go outside and give Hermes a good brushing to pass the time. Sometimes I'd let her run free around the snowy fields. And when she'd tired herself out, I'd go back indoors and scrub away at the tiny teacup stains I hadn't even noticed before.

Before I knew it, The Snail had gone into full-blown hibernation. The entire village's transportation had stopped because of the snow and customers from outside of town were no longer able to get here. There was still the minibus, of course. But instead of taking several sets of passengers a day, it was now doing only one run in the morning that didn't come back until the evening. So if anyone did want to come and visit, it would be easier for them to stay overnight.

As for me, I was still without a voice. I remember hearing somewhere that if you stop using one of your abilities, then that ability will gradually waste away. I'd been sitting eating instant noodles at the counter of Bar Amour once when I was still very young when a particularly drunk customer said to me, "Did you know that a transvestite's penis gets smaller and smaller all the time? It's because they never use it, you know."

I wondered if my voice had simply been exhausted and I felt that if I were to poke at my throat with a pair of tweezers then my voice might actually fall out of my body and abandon its home for ever. But even if that did ever happen, I wouldn't really mind. After all, I still had my cooking – my dearest ally. And you didn't need a voice for that.

When my mother returned, I was sorry to see that our relationship was just the same as it ever was, with the two of us acting like opposing sides in a cold war. I like to think of myself as the kind of person who can love pretty much any person or any living thing. I say "pretty much" because there was just one person whom I could never really like from the bottom of my heart, and that person was of course my mother. It was as if my dislike of her ran as deep as my love for everything else in this world. Unfortunately, it's impossible for people to keep the waters of their hearts clear and pure and everyone's becomes soiled with dirt at some stage. I'm sure even the most pious of saints has moments when he or she wants to shout out a stream of obscenities. Just as I'm sure that you can find a hint of pure compassion in the heart of even the hardest criminal on death row. Even if it took a microscope to find it.

In an attempt to keep the waters of my heart as clear as possible, I decided to remain silent. When fish swim around, they dislodge the silt on the river bottom and make the waters obscure. But if I could keep my heart and mind as serene as possible, then maybe all the silt would settle back to the bottom.

So I decided to be mindful of the silt when interacting with my mother; mindful of stirring the waters. Though some might say I started to ignore her completely, I prefer to think of it as giving her some space. A space for calm, where the waters could be serene and where the silt of my heart could settle.

The days drifted idly by until one exceptionally sunny January day when Kuma suddenly appeared at the café and said, "Ringo! Do you want to come with me to check out the home of the red radishes?"

It was all very sudden, but I figured it wasn't every day I could meet the grower of such wonderful radishes, and I wanted to express my gratitude in person for the ingredients that had made the dinner for the gay couple so special. So I decided to go along.

I quickly put on my red anorak, my dark-blue ski pants and my usual rain boots before leaving the house. Then we rode Kuma's snowmobile as far as we could, got off, put on our snowshoes and walked the rest of the way through the snow that stretched far into the distance. Our destination was a field that stretched across the slope on the other side of the Twin Peaks where the red radishes were resting beneath a thick layer of white snow.

"I wanted to show you this view at least once!" huffed Kuma as he tried to catch his breath. He was carrying a bag on his back that looked extremely heavy, but I had no idea what was inside. Off we went along the trail again, with Kuma in front and me following closely behind in complete silence, except for the squeaks that accompanied my footsteps in the snow, like the sound of a rabbit trying to escape from a hole somewhere.

The view consisted only of snow and ice for as far as you could see, with an ocean-blue sky above and just a few clouds sailing across its plain. Suddenly, Kuma stopped in his tracks and turned to face me.

"Snowdrops!" he said and pointed to the ground.

Looking in the direction of his gloved finger, I could see a small flower with its head bowed to the ground. Then another. Then another. In fact there were several patches of them all around.

"I planted these a few years back," said Kuma. "I'd wanted Siñorita to see them. But they never blossomed while she was here. Only once she was gone. But what pretty flowers they are."

We took a short break to enjoy the flowers. I couldn't help but notice how they looked like little fairies that had decided to pop their heads up from under the snow and I was hit by the wonder of life and how it can flourish with beauty, even in such a cold environment as this.

In the bare treetops above, birds were singing songs of love to one another and I drank in a deep breath of that pure mountain air. Then we continued on our hike down the small path along the riverside, with the occasional breeze caressing our faces with the slightest suggestion of the sweet scent of nature.

"We made it!" called out Kuma as we turned a corner to see a cabin standing alone on the hillside. A man around the same age as Kuma was waiting for us inside. This was the man who grew those special radishes and standing next to him was his wife, who was petite in stature and had a face almost identical to her husband's. The two of them had kept going the radish-growing business that had been in their family for generations.

Quickly, I reached into my basket and took out my notebook with the intention of writing a message of thanks for the radishes. But as I fumbled with my pencil, I realized my hands were far too cold to write. Fortunately, Kuma knew me well enough to know what I was trying to say, so he translated my silence into gratitude. Then he unpacked his backpack and I immediately understood why he'd been struggling to catch his breath before. He'd packed a lunch for all of us!

"You're always feeding me, Ringo," he said, pulling the lids off the Tupperware containers, one by one. "So I thought this would make a nice change!"

"They are all my mother's recipes," he continued, while carefully transferring the contents to plates. "So I don't know if you'll like them, but please try them."

There were mixed vegetables seasoned with soy sauce, rolled egg omelette, fried chicken, rice balls and various pickled vegetables. The way Kuma's mother flavoured the food was different from my grandmother's light seasoning, and from my mum's chemical-like seasoning too. The boiled potatoes, burdock root and carrots were all boiled to the point where they simply fell apart in the mouth. The soup stock seemed to be made only from dried sardines, and there were anchovies in the boiled vegetable dishes. The rolled egg had a firm texture and was seasoned with plenty of sugar and soy sauce. And inside the rice balls were big pieces of cooked cod roe.

With each and every bite, flavours burst forth and spread across my mouth. And though the dishes may have lacked the elegance or finish of a lunchbox prepared by some high-class restaurant, they more than made up for it in their sheer authenticity.

"Now this is what I call comfort food!" said the wife as she stuffed a big rice ball into her mouth, and I couldn't agree with her more. That's when I realized that it had been a while since I'd eaten anything that someone else had made!

The rice was cooked a little too soft for my liking, but that didn't stop me from munching down several mouthfuls and imagining their energy rising from the bottom of my stomach; the energy that had come from Kuma's mother as I'm sure she'd prepared them with her heart, her soul and kind thoughts for us. So I wasn't just eating rice. I was taking in her love.

A moment later, I felt myself overcome by a sense of nostalgia or déjà vu. I couldn't be sure which at first. I thought back to old memories of my grandmother and pictured her standing with her back to me in her clean and organized kitchen. The *obento* she used to make and the one Kuma's mum had made were suffused with the same spirit. And for a moment, while chewing on a piece of rice, I felt tears welling up in my eyes and fought to stop them from rolling down my cheeks. After drinking some *dokudami* tea that the wife had prepared, the four of us went outside and walked towards the radish fields. As we dug into the snow, the whiteness all around became flecked with red radish tops and I heard the farmer say that by keeping them under the snow, the radishes could be given a much sweeter flavour.

"Go on, try one," he said, handing Kuma and I a radish each. I bit into it, finding it so juicy that I worried its juice might squirt everywhere! Its scent was so surprisingly fresh and its flavour was a perfect balance of sweet and spicy. We were told that we could eat as many as we liked, so both Kuma and I indulged ourselves. I was amazed to find, for the first time in my life, that a farmer can grow a whole crop of radishes in a single field in the same way, yet each and every radish could develop something unique in its flavour.

As we made our way back, we could see through the snow-covered trees to the ocean in the distance. The straight line where the sky met the water seemed to go on for ever. On one rather steep point, I lost my footing and fell on my backside.

"Are you OK?" said Kuma, hurrying back in my direction. But I wasn't hurt. Only a little embarrassed. So I stuck out my tongue at him and gave a playful laugh. Then I grabbed Kuma's shoulders and tried to get up. But I couldn't! It was as if I couldn't muster any strength in my legs and I found myself crumpling back down onto the snow. I was sure I hadn't broken anything. But there was a good chance I might have sprained my ankle.

"Ringo, hold this!" said Kuma as he took off his backpack, which was now much lighter than before.

"C'mon, get on," he said. "I'm still strong enough to carry someone your size!"

Hesitantly, I leant against Kuma's back and put my arms around his neck.

"Here we go!" he called out as he got up slowly. And the next moment, I was taking in a familiar view, only from a slightly higher vantage point. As he started to walk along with me on his back, I thought back to myself as a child, crying in the hallway of the elementary school until Kuma had come by, put me on his back like this, and whisked me away to the janitor's room to show me the Yamane sound asleep inside a pot.

Since then, I'd grown into a woman, moved to the city, found a boyfriend, had my heart broken and finally become the owner of The Snail. I'd experienced so many things in my life, but here I was back in the same situation as in my childhood, with my arms around dear Kuma. He was always there for me, always taking care of me, and all I ever did was cause him trouble. Even now, as he selflessly carried me along, he did so without any regard at all for his bad leg.

Oh Kuma, why are you always so nice to me? I said to myself in my mind. And with perfect timing, Kuma said quietly. "This is the least I can do. Mama-san helped me so much by listening to my complaints so patiently."

By "Mama-san" he meant the "Mama-san" of Bar Amour. My mum.

"After Siñorita left, it was a rough time for me," he continued. "I drank too much, and sometimes took it out on Mama-San. But Mama-San would always listen with a smile on her face. And though I said a lot of bad things, she was always willing to forgive and forget."

Then Kuma told me something I never knew.

"Even on that day when I saw you again," he said. "Mama had called saying you were back and she asked me to go help you out. She said you were probably up the fig tree and asked me to go check on you. So I went, and what a surprise. There you were, just as she'd said. She's really something, you know. I can't thank her enough."

I felt as if a small sour plum had been pushed into my mouth. I'd had no idea. I thought I'd met Kuma purely by chance that day when actually it was my mum who'd brought him back into my life. With that realization, the pain in my ankle subsided, only to be replaced by a burning in my heart.

Somehow, we made it back to the truck safely and as we drove along the familiar road we'd followed on the way here, Kuma said, "Ringo, why don't you have a soak in the hot springs? It might help your ankle. I'll make sure nobody else comes. I promise not to peek either. So what do you say?"

I looked at Kuma with his sincere face and thought about his suggestion. The hot springs on the outskirts of town were open to both men and women and I'd heard stories many times of how their waters were good for healing sprains and bruises. I was feeling a little chilly too. So I took my notebook from the basket, wrote on it and showed Kuma.

Thank you. You must be cold too. Why don't you join me?

Kuma read the note, gave a slight nod and took the next right turn to head us towards the springs.

When we arrived there, the sun was already beginning to set. I really hoped we'd be lucky enough to be the only ones there. After all, there's nothing worse than being stuck in a hot spring with a bunch of old grandpas in the middle of a gossip session. Soon, before I knew it, the sun had set completely, leaving a delicate bluish-white glow from the snow as our only illumination.

In the middle of February, my mum invited me to a party. I'd returned from finishing my preparations for making Korean kimchi to find a note in her handwriting pinned to the gate of Hermes's pen. It was an invitation to the annual blowfish party at the Bar Amour and it was being organized by Neocon. The guest list comprised about six or seven Bar Amour regulars as well as Mum and Neocon and there were several other guests who had gone to Hawaii with Mum over the New Year's holidays.

Though Neocon was the president of a construction company, he somehow held the necessary licence for preparing the poisonous blowfish in a safe way. I couldn't make up my mind whether to attend or not until the day of the party – a decision made more difficult by the fact that I had no customer bookings for the eatery that night and therefore the rare chance of a quiet night where I could knit or relax with a book. More than that, I wanted to avoid seeing my mum being all flirty and affectionate with her lover. But in the end, my passion for cuisine won over and I was drawn by the desire to taste the blowfish.

I'd eaten blowfish, or *fugu* as we call it, on a couple of occasions before, but since it was traditionally sliced paper thin, I'd found it difficult to really taste anything. Nevertheless, it was a dish that seemed to be all the rage among top TV chefs around the world. So I guess my objective in attending the party was to try to understand all the fuss about *fugu*.

At around five in the afternoon, I heard a racket outside and stepped out to investigate. Neocon was struggling to tie a white horse to a palm tree, which meant he'd made a conscious decision to leave his beloved Mercedes behind and drink a skinful of alcohol.

"I heard you got robbed by Ali Baba!" he called out to me.

I could only imagine that my mum had told him about what happened with my Indian boyfriend and that the both of them had found it rather amusing. How nice to have that thrown in my face all over again, just as I'd started to put it behind me!

Rather than retaliate, I simply stepped back inside Bar Amour and started chopping some Hakata spring onions. Neocon, who'd followed me inside, started taking out the ingredients I'd partially prepared back home and lined them up, one by one, on the counter. Neocon had had the *fugu* delivered all the way from Oita prefecture and you could tell how fresh it was just by looking at it.

After removing its poisonous parts, Neocon pulled out a knife made especially for the preparation of *fugu* and started to cut thin slices of sashimi, while I poured Neocon's home-made *ponzu* sauce into a shallow dish for each guest. Eventually, when all the guests had arrived, we all sat down around the plate of prepared *fugu* and the party began. Everyone had brought plenty of alcohol and we went through one bottle before enjoying the next, drinking sake, shochu, beer and wine. Neocon had also brought along some champagne. Not just any champagne, but a bottle of Cristal rosé. Mum's favourite champagne! I'd only ever seen a bottle of Cristal once before in a classy imported-goods store and I had no idea how it tasted. All I knew was that this sophisticated and very expensive champagne was outside chilling in the snow in preparation for the delights it would release later.

The slices of raw *fugu*, prepared just a little thicker than usual, had the same fleeting beauty as a light snowfall. When they were grilled, they became juicier with a more pronounced flavour where the meat met the bones. And when they were fried, they took on an interesting texture with a little more chewiness than one might expect of fish. It seemed everyone was so focused on enjoying the fish that they all forgot to make any conversation and I too felt as if my whole body had been turned into one giant tongue. I was in a state of pure Epicurean bliss, as if invited to some heavenly banquet in a delightful dream.

Finally, it was the moment everyone had been waiting for all night – the liver roulette! The levels of poison in the liver of the *fugu* varied from fish to fish and we took a little of it to garnish what was left of the sashimi. Apparently,

131

this was really only allowed in Oita prefecture. But everyone ate this in secret every year at my mum's party anyway, and fortunately there'd been no fatalities so far.

There was even a kind of method to this madness. The first time they'd held one of these parties at Bar Amour, they'd eaten the first serving of *fugu* along with the liver. After that, everyone had agreed that it would be so unfortunate if one were to drop dead after only the first course and miss out on the grilled *fugu*, the fried *fugu* and the rice porridge made with the leftovers. So they came up with the idea of preparing two plates of sashimi instead – one prepared in the normal way for the first course, and one prepared with the liver as the last course. In this way, there was still the chance of dying, but not until you'd had chance to enjoy every course of the meal. How greedy is that!

"Chaaampaagnee!" called out my inebriated mother, prompting a round of applause from everyone at the table. Then Neocon stood up and went outside to retrieve the Cristal from the snow. When he came back in, I noticed that for some reason he seemed to be hiding the bottle, wrapping it in a page of old newspaper that bore a picture of a baseball player with one arm raised in the air.

Neocon went behind the counter and Mum went to join him so they could prepare for a toast. Meanwhile, the course of liver roulette was ready on the table. Everyone seemed pretty drunk, and from the corner of my eye I stole glances at Neocon and Mum, who seemed to be acting a little suspiciously. Unfortunately, my suspicions were confirmed when I noticed how they were preparing the drinks – keeping the bottle out of proper sight so they could pour themselves a glass of Cristal but pour some cheap cava for everyone else. Suddenly, the party didn't seem so much fun any more and I even started to feel a little sick in the stomach.

As my mum started handing out the glasses of champagne, I did my best to keep an innocent smile on my face. If you took the trouble to look, you could see the difference in the shades of rosé, but it seemed everyone else was far too drunk to notice. But why should they? Surely nobody would expect them to do something so cheap and selfish.

When my mum had gone around the table and handed a glass to me, I took it while making no effort to hide my disapproval. Then I noticed the shade of rosé in my glass and was immediately confused.

"Don't bother yourself about it," my mum whispered to me. "Just enjoy it."

Before I could say anything in response, Neocon – the host of tonight's party – stood up and said, "What better way than this to spend your final moments. Thank you everyone, for everything. And cheers to you all!"

Then he placed a generous chunk of liver on a sliver of *fugu* sashimi and carried it to his mouth. Then, just as I was wishing that the liver would kill him, he yelled out loud, "It's safe!"

"Too bad," I thought to myself as I heaved a sigh.

Rather than dwell on my feelings, I decided to try and wash away my disappointment by knocking back my first ever glass of Cristal. Of course, I did feel a little bad for the others. But then, it wasn't every day you got a chance to try something like this. So in the battle between my curiosity and my conscience, my curiosity was triumphant.

After saying a quick apology to the other guests in my mind, I carried the beautiful pink champagne to my mouth. With the first sip and every sip thereafter, I felt as if a flower-filled meadow was spreading throughout my body. And though I'd never had a clear idea of what heaven might look like, I could picture people being given a sip of this as they arrived at the pearly gates.

As we moved on to a course of *fugu* soup, the party still seemed far from ending. We'd added rice to the soup to make a kind of congee. And when we'd finished eating that, the drinks started flowing again and the party seemed to catch its second wind.

People drank, sang and made a lot of noise. While some were belting out karaoke songs, others were crashed out on the floor. While one man slurred earnestly about world affairs, the person sitting next to him was checking the weather on TV. Everyone seemed to be having the time of their lives.

I went to stand alone at the counter and began to clean up. It simply wasn't in my nature to be able to leave dirty dishes lying around. And my mum, who was now clearly wasted with her head propped up on Neocon's shoulder, was in no state to help. For a moment, I watched them sitting together, leaning sloppily into each other like two different flavours of melting ice cream. Then I distracted myself with the dishes again in an attempt to take my mind off their canoodling.

From where I was standing, I could hear Neocon whispering into my mum's ear, while stroking her thigh.

"C'mon Ruriko, I think it's time you let me take you for a roll in the hay. Come on, I treated you to the *fugu*, didn't I? And you enjoyed that fancy Cristal, right? So what do you say?"

"Booo!" cooed back my mum, imitating the buzzer that accompanied the wrong answer in TV game shows.

"Oh come on! What have you got to lose? Nobody knows the future. For all we know, this could be the last ever opportunity we have to be together."

At first, I thought they were acting out some sort of comic routine. After all, ever since I was a child, everyone knew Neocon was Mum's lover. So it was almost impossible to believe that they'd actually never been intimate.

As I stood there bewildered, Neocon suddenly spoke to me.

"Hey," he said, in a menacing voice. "Talk to your mum, will you? Tell her to give the nice Mr Neocon a good time for once in her life!"

Obviously offended, I glared back at Neocon without saying a word. But he was clearly unperturbed and just tutted and continued.

"What is it with you and your mum anyway? You're both so damn stubborn. Like mother, like daughter. They're only legs, you know. So just spread them and let me in. She's too stubborn to show me a good time and you're too stubborn to even speak!"

Suddenly, one of the regular customers who'd been belting out a rendition of 'Amagi Goe' joined in on the conversation with the microphone still in hand.

"Hey, let it go, will you!" boomed his voice. "I don't know what kind of woman you think she is, but I'll have you know that Ruriko is a pure and precious woman. A woman who values her virginity. She should be protected, like a national treasure. There are too many young women who'll jump into bed with anyone without a second thought. But she's not like that!"

After his outburst, the salaryman in a suit stood there for several moments, seemingly intoxicated by the brilliance of his speech until the backing track for his song ended. As for me, I was completely confused. Why on earth would he call my mum a virgin? And if that was true, then she wasn't even really my mum. I'd always been at least a little suspicious that this might be the case, especially since the two of us were so very different. So perhaps my suspicion had been right all along. Perhaps I had a more compassionate, kinder-hearted mother living somewhere else in the world. Perhaps she was even searching for me. I started to allow my dream to fill my heart with hope. But in a second, my bubble of hope was burst.

"You were my immaculate conception!" said my inebriated mother with her face as pink as the Cristal in her glass. She'd always had the annoying habit of telling ludicrous lies when she got too drunk and it had been a bad habit that had tricked a number of men over the years. I stood there for a moment, wondering what she would say next, when the salaryman in the suit chimed in again.

"Did you honestly not know about this, Ringo?" he said with bulging eyes.

What on earth were they talking about? I felt like kicking the kitchen counter.

Neocon was already fast asleep and snoring like Hermes. Mum, on the other hand, was clearly drunk, but very much awake. She looked me straight in the face and said, "You, Ringo, are a water-pistol baby."

I felt as if a bucket of plaster had been poured into my brain.

"Everybody knows that story around here," said the salaryman, placing the mike down on the table and taking a seat near the counter to fill me in on the details. Then he embarked on a story that left me completely speechless.

It was a story that went something like this.

Mum had been engaged to her high-school boyfriend who was a year older than she was. The two were strongly drawn to each other and they'd promised each other they'd spend their lives together, but that they'd keep their relationship platonic until they'd graduated from high school. Mum's fiancé was a good student, and following graduation he went off to study medicine at a university in Osaka. So for a while they had a long-distance relationship that consisted only of letters.

Mum studied hard so she could be closer to her fiancé and succeeded in getting into a junior college in Kyoto. But when she found her way to the address she'd been writing to, her fiancé had already moved. She never saw him again.

But the story didn't end there.

After that, Mum entered a self-destructive phase. In the hopes of somehow getting over her fiancé and starting a completely new life, she decided to get pregnant. But because she couldn't be impregnated by her dear fiancé, she took the reckless attitude that anyone would do. At least, that was how she felt for a while. She soon came to her senses a little and decided that wasn't a good idea. So instead she started to wonder if there was any way she could become pregnant while still remaining a virgin. This is what inspired her to use a water pistol.

"They didn't have sperm banks back in those days," Mum interrupted.

"Or even today," added the salaryman. "You know they're still illegal in Japan."

Anyway, Mum chose her partner from one of her transient romances, like drawing a ticket in a raffle. Then she took the man's sperm and poured it into a water pistol, which she then inserted inside herself and squirted, Mum explained, using hand gestures I could have done without.

"I think he was married. He had a ring on his ring finger. That's why your name is Rinko. Rin for *furin* as in affair. So Rinko basically means love child. Isn't that right?" Mum asked one of the older regulars who was still glued to the weather on TV.

139

"Your mum is a devoted lady," came the voice from the old man, who managed to reply without shifting his gaze from the impending typhoon on the screen.

"That's right! And I'm going to stay a virgin until I die!" shouted Mum, jumping up from her seat and raising an arm in the air like the Statue of Liberty, before collapsing onto the counter face first and falling straight to sleep.

I guess I was in shock. If what I'd just been told was true, then this was a serious matter indeed. I've never heard of someone conceiving a child via a sperm-filled water pistol, but if it really was the case, then I must surely be the world's first ever water-pistol baby!

By now, Bar Amour had turned into a place of peace and quiet. Grandpa Owl had called out his midnight hoot some time ago, some of the customers had paid and left, and there were several others passed out on the floor, so I had to do my best to clean the place up without disturbing them.

I'd always been a bit gullible, so I still wasn't sure if I was the butt of some stupid joke that everyone else in the room was in on. But there was something about it that made me feel this wasn't the case this time. Somewhere in my heart, I was already beginning to realize that despite their appearances, each and every person in this room was both serious and sensitive. It was as if tonight I'd caught a glimpse of a different mum in another world. A mum who smelt just a little sweeter than the one I was used to.

The peace and quiet in Bar Amour didn't last for long. I was standing there replaying the water-pistol story in my mind when all of a sudden, Neocon got up and said, "Gotta piss." Then he opened the door and stepped outside, though I don't know why. There was a perfectly good toilet inside the bar.

When Neocon came back in a minute later, he was shivering with cold as he fumbled to fasten his zipper. Then he looked me in the eye and said, "You threw out the wreath of flowers I sent as an opening gift, didn't you?"

I thought back to the day when I'd received the flowers and moved them to the back of Bar Amour. Unfortunately, I hadn't moved them away since.

"It's like you're pissing on my good wishes!" spat Neocon. "Anyway, I'm hungry. Make me something to eat!"

But I didn't feel like making anything for Neocon. And why should I? I tend to cook only for people I actually care for. So I pretended not to hear him. But then his voice took on a nastier tone.

"So you refuse to cook for people you don't like, huh?" he said, with a gangster-like voice as he blew smoke in my face. "Who the hell d'you think you are anyway? The big-shot owner and chef of Café Escargot! Think you're a professional, do you? Well professionals don't have the luxury of going round hand-picking their customers, do they! You're just playing house in there. Like some egocentric feminist extravaganza. Well it's time for you to wake up to yourself. Get real. Now go and make me something to eat!"

By the time Neocon had finished speaking, he had two big spit bubbles at the corners of his mouth that looked like the foam on grasshopper eggs. I wanted to shout back at him, to tell him my place was called The Snail and not Café Escargot! And who was he to call me some sort of egotistical feminist? I was just passionate about my cooking, that's all. Like any first-rate chef should be. If only I had a large knife to hand, I'd show him a thing or two. After all, he wasn't only insulting me – he was insulting the god of cooking! But rather than shout out in protest, I pulled the fridge door open with a rough tug. But what awaited me inside was pitiful. All I could see was some leftover miso and nothing else I could use at all. I knew there wasn't much in the eatery either since I kept my stock to a minimum during the quiet winter season. But my reputation was on the line here, so I couldn't back down.

Keeping a straight face, I scurried off to The Snail. Surely there would be something there I could use. Something that would shut Neocon's stupid mouth. Once inside the eatery, I rummaged through all my cabinets, but there simply wasn't anything I could use. I didn't even have anything in Grandma's pickle jar and the kimchi I'd prepared the other day was nowhere near ready. It was also way past the closing time of the local Yorozuya supermarket and there weren't any all-night shops in town. Realizing my lack of options, I realized that unfortunately I would have to apologize to Neocon. But when I opened the drawer with my stationery in it, there was a brownish block sitting at the back of it. I picked it up wondering what on earth it could be, and discovered it was the dried bonito I'd misplaced. I'd originally stored it in the top drawer, but it must've fallen down to the drawer below. That's when an idea came to me. There was still some of the rice we'd cooked for the blowfish porridge at Bar Amour. So I could get some quality soup stock if I used this dried bonito to make a simple *ochazuke* by putting the leftover rice in it. Immediately I started shaving the dried bonito, and after going through the cabinets some more, I was also able to find some dried seaweed.

After a lot of frantic movement, I ran back to Bar Amour with the bowl of shaved bonito and dried seaweed in my hands. Then I boiled some water in a deep aluminium pan as Neocon watched my every move with his stupid bloated face.

Then he spat out his next round of abuse.

143

"Listen girly," he said. "I've been to practically every renowned restaurant around the world. Once I even went all the way to Tanzania to eat a hippo stew. So you'd better brace yourself. If I think it tastes like crap, I won't hesitate to tell you so. Just don't cry when you hear what I think of your cooking."

To tell the truth, I was so terrified that my legs were shaking. But I did my best to concentrate on making the soup from the dried bonito, allowing Neocon's words to go in my left ear and straight out of the right. I'd heard about the hippo stew so many times since I was a child. For a while, I heard nothing else from him other than his repetitious explanation of how hippo meat was "like an exquisite, juicier version of beef". But for the moment, it was important for me to clear my mind of such useless thoughts. It was painful to have to cook for a man I despised so much. So I tried my hardest not to think about it. Because if I were to dwell on my hatred for him, it would surely be reflected in the taste of the dish. So instead, I simply emptied my heart and mind.

My grandmother had always told me how important it is to fill one's heart with happy and peaceful thoughts when preparing food and I took another deep breath to bring my feelings under control. I focused my attention on finding the precise moment to take the *kombu* seaweed out of the pot. Then I waited several moments before introducing the bonito. Just as that comforting, familiar scent began to reach my nose, I turned the heat down just a touch. It was all going smoothly so far. All that was left to do now was to adjust the flavour with salt. That's when I realized that my tongue had completely lost its sense of taste!

Perhaps it was because I'd had so much to eat and quite a bit to drink. Usually, I'd know how to season a dish with a single taste, but on this occasion it didn't seem to matter how much salt I added, it always seemed to be both too salty and not salty enough at the same time. It was like trying to find my way through a forest in the middle of the night while wearing a blindfold.

In front of me, I could see Neocon shaking his legs impatiently and I knew that the longer I kept him waiting, the more likely he was to spit out some spiteful comment. So I decided to trust my heart and add just one more pinch of salt. Then I placed some rice from the cooker into a warm bowl I'd prepared earlier, poured the freshly prepared soup from above and completed the dish. There was also a tiny bit of chopped Hakata onion left over from earlier, so I sprinkled it on top to finish.

I used both hands to place the dish in front of Neocon together with a pair of chopsticks. Then, looking Neocon in the eyes, I said "Go ahead" with my facial expression only. Because I was a little tipsy, I was able to be much bolder than normal, which was fortunate because – unlike

ITO OGAWA

at The Snail – I couldn't retreat to steal glances from
behind the curtain.

Without a moment's pause, Neocon picked up his chopsticks and dug in. He was sitting just a metre in front of
where I was standing, and though I was nervous there was
nowhere I could hide and nothing I could do. Nothing,
except wait for the moment of truth, that is.

Though I wasn't yet sure of the taste, the scent of the
soup was unmistakably beautiful and Neocon's slurps re-
verberated around the room. I felt as if the nervousness of
my entire life had been condensed into one single incident
and I closed my eyes to compose myself. Then eventually,
Neocon stopped eating and placed the chopsticks down by
the side of the bowl. On opening my eyes, I saw an empty
bowl in front of him. In fact, it was so empty, it looked as
if it had already been rinsed clean.

"That was good. Thank you," he said, with eyes that
were surprisingly red and teary. He was a man with no
reservations about making the most distasteful remarks
and jokes that no one found amusing. But he was not a
man to give a compliment out of pure politeness. Immediately, I felt a rush of emotion to my heart and I ran to
the toilet where Neocon wouldn't see my tears.

After dabbing my eyes with my apron, I composed
myself and came out. Unfortunately, Neocon had already
gone. But in addition to the 10,000-yen he'd left for the

146

party, there was another 10,000 yen note placed under the rice bowl. The two notes were laid out neatly in the shape of a V. I stepped outside, hoping to catch him before he got too far, only to find a trail of horseshoe prints along the path of snow that glowed a light blue in the moonlight.

I went back inside, finding Mum coughing in her sleep, so I gently placed her fur coat on her shoulders. Now there was only her and myself left in Bar Amour and the faintest trace of her perfume. I thought to myself how I didn't hate that scent as much as I once thought I had. Then I looked at Mum's sleeping face again. She looked tired out, that was for sure. But there was something in the way she looked that made me worry that she might not be well.

As I was just about to leave, my mum began to mumble some words in her sleep. And though I couldn't be sure of what she'd said, the sound of her words seemed to cover my shoulders like a warm veil and I took those words as my second sign of gratitude for the night.

When I stepped out again, I found myself in the middle of a snowstorm. The snowy season was definitely here and the wind was raging like a crazed witch, flinging snow and ice into my face that stung like hot chilli powder. But I knew that soon the ice would thaw and spring would come again. Beautiful flowers would come into bloom and we'd soon be smiling among the myriad floral aromas.

Perhaps there was even a chance that the relationship between Mum and Neocon would blossom too.

Despite the biting wind around me, I stood with my heart full of hope. But I didn't let down my guard. Hope, after all, had a habit of being cut away from me in an instant, as if severed by some unseen guillotine.

I'd been feeling dreary all day. I'd started the morning by burning the bread for Hermes's breakfast. Then, on the way to the eatery, I'd accidentally stepped on a couple of butterflies – killing them as they slumbered in the snow. Both of these things were nothing more than careless accidents, but they continued to bother me throughout the day.

My bad luck continued in the afternoon. As I was preparing an *acqua pazza* as requested by the customer for that day, I had trouble removing the insides of the flounder. Usually I was able to remove the insides in one chunk by sticking my finger in the gills and pulling down and outward, but on this particular day the insides came out in bits. I also dropped and broke the special bottle of extra-virgin olive oil that I'd ordered from Italy, and I cut my finger on the glass when I was picking the pieces off the floor. It was as if the god of cooking had given up on me. The ultimate blow, however, was my mum's confession.

I'd decided to take a bath after I'd returned home late at night from The Snail, when, without any warning, the door to the bath opened and Mum walked in stark naked! Startled, I froze in place. Mum would always go to work at Bar Amour in the evenings, so I had no recollection of ever taking a bath with her even as a child. So it was no surprise that I found myself reflexively tucking my knees together and covering my breasts with my hands like a teenager. But Mum didn't seem to even notice. She just said:

"I have something to tell you. Do you mind?"

After she'd splashed some bath water over her body in the wash basin, she squeezed herself into the tub next to me, causing a torrent of water to flow over the sides. I tried to step out, but Mum put a firm hand on my shoulders to tell me to stay.

"The other day, I ran into Shu," she began, with her face glowing.

I didn't have my notebook on me. The bath was the one place I didn't bring it with me. So all I could do was listen.

"You heard what was said at the *fugu* party, didn't you? He was my first love and we were engaged to be married. But then, you know…" said Mum in a weary tone. She sounded so different, so drained, that I felt a little uneasy and couldn't help but watch her face for some sort of sign. But without looking back at my face, she carried on talking as if into the distance and I started to wonder if she might finally be going mad.

"Shu hadn't changed one bit," she said. "Of course, we've both aged a little over the thirty years since we last met. But deep inside, he's still the same old Shu."

I looked at my mum's neck, noticing it was slightly red, like a ripe peach. All this news was coming so suddenly and I was starting to feel a little dizzy. So I decided to stand up. I figured I could get the rest of her story later on. But in the moments that followed, everything changed. It was as if the blade of some huge guillotine had been brought down on my life.

As her story unfurled, I felt overcome by the need to get out of the bath. So I jumped out and crouched down with only a towel wrapped around myself as I struggled to digest what she'd just told me. But no matter how many times I repeated her words in my head, I couldn't quite believe it. To think that my own mum had cancer. To think she only had a few months to live. To think that she'd run into the same doctor who'd been her precious first love. And to hear her say that she felt fortunate and happy from the bottom of her heart, despite living on borrowed time, because she'd finally been reunited with her soulmate.

It was a love story too incredible even for an afternoon soap opera and I couldn't believe such a story could happen in the twenty-first century. In my eyes, Mum was a tough, harsh character whom I was constantly fighting with. I'd never once seen her cry. In fact, I used to believe she was immortal. She was like a sandbag that never broke, no matter how many times you might punch it. So it seemed somehow ridiculous that such an unusually strong-willed woman could fall victim to such a common disease.

I took a step towards the fridge and opened the door, letting the bright lemon light sting my eyes like eye drops. There was a familiar half-empty jar of margarine that I recognized from before I'd ever left home. Only now it was covered with a carpet of mould. So I opened the container of marmalade next to it, but that was also covered in mould. There was even a dead cockroach in the fridge between the half-used ketchup and the mayonnaise – all characteristic signs of my mum's disorganized life. But if Mum was dying, then soon all these things would disappear from the world, and that was a thought that made me want to scream.

That night, I couldn't sleep at all. I threw a down jacket on over my pyjamas and stepped outside to where thousands of stars sparkled in the cold night sky. I wished I had some company, but there was no one I could go to. So instead I went to Hermes. The heavy night air clung to my skin like a sea cucumber and I felt as if I was being slowly immersed from the tips of my nails into thick, sweet *yokan* liquid until it became difficult to breathe. I still struggled to believe what my mum had told me and

151

ITO OGAWA

I wanted so much to believe it was merely another one of her bad jokes.

When I reached Hermes's pen, she was already wide awake. Perhaps she was having trouble sleeping too. Or perhaps she could even sense what was happening. After running up to greet me like a dog, Hermes stared at me with her tiny eyes and tilted her head to the side. She looked so much cuter in the moonlight than in daylight and I couldn't help but put my arms around her back and give her a big hug. Her body was warm, and though to most people she surely couldn't have smelt good at all, to me she smelt like a grassy meadow. Then she pushed her nose against my ear and breathed heavily, tickling me so much I almost laughed out loud.

There are so many things in this world that are beyond the control of mere individuals. In fact, the things that are within our control are actually very few and far between. It's as if for the most part, we are merely tossed this way and that by some great unseen river, with no regard for our hopes and dreams. It also seems to me that there are more bad things than good things in life. In my life, this was especially true. Still, I'd always made a concerted effort to fully appreciate the good things whenever they happened. But now, the more I thought about it, the more depressed I became, until I felt so bad I almost bit right through my lip.

The next morning, Hermes got diarrhoea for the first time since I'd been there. Her tail, which was normally wound like a spring, was simply dangling like a rope and I rushed to get her logbook. Thumbing through the pages of Mum's beautiful handwriting, I found a page that said, "In case of diarrhoea, mix two to three tablespoons of powdered charcoal with an equal amount of food." I tried it straight away, but wondered if her sickness was born of concern for my mum rather than any stomach sickness.

I spent every night after that lying in my futon or next to Hermes with my eyes wide open. My body was completely exhausted, but I couldn't fall sleep once I started thinking about everything. I seemed to be completely lethargic and uninterested in doing anything at all. And though I repeatedly promised myself I would spend my days by my weakening mum's side, I actually ended up opening The Snail as usual. I guess on some level I was scared that if I didn't open the eatery now, then perhaps I never would again. Besides, seeing the happy faces of my customers was the only thing that kept me going.

There were plenty of fun times too, though. As spring approached, Kuma started receiving several phone calls a day on his mobile phone from people enquiring about The Snail or wanting to make a reservation. Momo, the high-school student who'd saved up her pocket money to come last year in the hope of confessing her love to the boy she liked, came again with her new boyfriend. The farmer's son and the teacher who were some of the very first guests of the eatery came by to show me their wedding pictures. The Mistress came by with her new, younger boyfriend. There was also Kozue, who came along with her mother one day when her father was away on business, although this time she didn't bring the rabbit.

In the beginning, many customers had been attracted by rumours of The Snail as the place where dreams come true. Nowadays, people were returning because they simply wanted to eat here again. It appeared that I had become one of their regular restaurants, and there was no greater honour for a chef that I could think of.

The seasons seemed to rush by so quickly and I felt an urgency to go and harvest the butterbur and wild asparagus while they were still at their best. But it was difficult to keep up with the mountains that were literally brimming with springtime treasures such as honewort, horsetail, mugwort, dandelions, *tara* buds and bracken.

Fortunately, Mum seemed to be doing OK, and she continued to stand behind the counter of Bar Amour, wearing brightly coloured outfits and too much make-up as always. She never told anyone she was sick and she refused to show any signs of pain whenever she took a step out of the house. She was so much more of a professional than I could ever be.

154

Just a few days after Mum had made her confession to me, she visited The Snail with her first love and current fiancé in tow. His name was Shuichi and he had the air of an elite doctor – with his lofty stature and city sophistication. But there was also a side of him that was more akin to a monk. It was obvious he wasn't my father, but he did highlight a connection between my mum and me. Though he wasn't young by any stretch, he was still breathtakingly handsome; so much so that my mother got all flustered whenever he was around. It was nice to learn that Mum and I shared something after all – a terrible weakness for strikingly good-looking men.

I brewed some Vietnamese lotus tea for them and let the two cups steep on the counter, giving out a gentle, sweet steam. It seemed Shuichi had spent a lot of time abroad. In fact, he was so different from Mum that it crossed my mind that he might even be a con man who makes his living by preying on moneyed women of a certain age. But I knew that was nonsense – Shuichi was a genuine catch. That was for sure.

He was a very serious person and he spoke passionately about how much he loved my mum and how the two of them had first met. He was a wonderful person, and like my mum, he was still single. He said he'd tried dating a few women after being separated from my mum, but none of those relationships had led to marriage. He said

155

it was because he simply couldn't forget my mum. But since he at least admitted to having some girlfriends over the years, I thought it best not to assume that he was still a virgin too. Not that it mattered at all; not at their age.

When he reached the end of his story, Shuichi paused, sat up straight, fixed his eyes on mine and said in a clear voice, "I would like to ask your permission to take Ruri-chan, no, Ruriko-san's hand in marriage. I promise to make your mother happy."

I don't know what had suddenly come over him, but he'd got down on his knees on the floor of the eatery and was now giving me a deep and sincere bow. Immediately, I rushed over to help him back to his feet. He seemed to be on the brink of tears, as was my mum, and I was totally lost for words. Until now, I'd been struggling to come to terms with the fact that my mum was locked in battle with a terrible disease, so I hadn't given any thought to anything beyond that. But there was absolutely no reason in the world why that should stop her from marrying, so I pulled out my notebook from the drawer and began to write in big letters.

Thank you, Shuichi. Please take good care of her.

As I handed Shuichi the note, I thought I was going to cry too. I wondered if perhaps this is the way fathers feel when they give a daughter away at the altar and it was funny to see all three of us trying so hard not to let our emotions overwhelm us.

The preparations for the wedding proceeded at a tremendous pace. Mum began research into all the things she wanted as a bride and the table in the living room became covered with magazine cut-outs of wedding dresses and catalogues of branded goods that could be handed out to the guests. She was happier than I think she'd ever been in her life and it was obvious for anyone to see.

Shuichi found time in his busy schedule at the hospital to visit Mum as often as he could. He'd bring herbal medicines to relieve her pain, give her massages and listen to her complaints while I prepared healthy brown rice in her kitchen. At times he'd even sit at the counter of Bar Amour and sip on a glass of shochu, or lend a hand in the kitchen by cooking sardines for the regular customers.

On the days where I finished early at The Snail, I went over to help out at Bar Amour. Mum had made no secret of the fact that she'd got engaged, and when she introduced Shuichi to her customers they all congratulated him heartily. They never spent a single night together, however, and they didn't move in together either. Instead, this pair of fifty-something lovebirds decided to stay faithful to their original promise of keeping their relationship platonic until the day of their wedding. And on hearing that, I no longer doubted that my mum might be a virgin.

One day, some weeks later, I awoke to find that my customers for that day had unexpectedly cancelled, leaving me with a day to relax. I decided to sleep in a little before getting up to prepare Hermes's bread and I was just taking a leisurely bath when I noticed Mum standing in a daze on the other side of the glass door.

In the weeks that had gone by, she'd started to look quite frail. In fact, she was starting to resemble a winter branch and I was afraid that a strong gust of wind might be enough to snap her in two. Shuichi was a specialist in palliative care and my mum refused all forms of surgery, anti-cancer drugs and chemotherapy. Instead she wanted only traditional remedies and there was nothing I could do to convince her otherwise. She weakly crouched on the floor on the other side of the glass door and said in a soft voice, "I have a favour to ask of you. I want you to organize my wedding reception."

The wedding was to be held with just the bride and groom present at the chapel of the hospital where Shuichi worked, with a large reception scheduled to take place at a nearby farm and I immediately thought she meant that they wanted me to do the catering. Then she surprised me with the next part of her request.

"I thought we'd eat Hermes. She'd like that too. Otherwise she'll be so sad when I'm gone. Do you think you could do that for me? It's my last wish."

So one beautiful spring day, Kuma and I tied a rope and dog leash around Hermes's neck and took her on a walk. The sun was smiling brightly in the blue sky and baby birds were flapping their wings on their way to the white clouds, but in our hearts we felt the darkness of the sombre task ahead of us.

Somewhere above us, there were thin icicles shaped like old ladies' breasts that were beating out a distinctive water-drop rhythm. It was a rhythm that made me think of the many times I'd heard Hermes's steps, caught wind of her smell and kneaded the bread she loved so much. She'd become like a sister to me and I couldn't help but picture her smile. Surely Mum must have felt the same way too.

Though Mum had originally joked about butchering Hermes by herself, it was a different matter when the time actually came.

Are you sure you want to do this?

I wrote in my notebook many times to confirm. But every time, Mum just answered in a weak, grandmother-like voice. "Yes, please go ahead."

At the time when she'd first asked me to prepare Hermes, Mum had talked about having a professional photographer take their portrait together first. But in the end, she'd found it more fitting to simply visit Hermes in her pen after everyone was asleep. From my window, I watched her go to Hermes, give her a loving kiss, and wrap her arms around that large, warm back. Then she fed her a loaf of her favourite sesame bread and returned to the house – leaving Hermes to munch away contentedly. That morning, Mum stayed in her bedroom until late. It was the last time Mum and Hermes spent time together.

As I tottered along the mountain path, I looked into Hermes's sunken eyes. For a moment, it looked as if she was laughing, or rather trying to force herself to laugh so as not to burst out crying. I felt I was probably just as confused as poor Hermes. I didn't know whether I was doing the right thing or the wrong thing, and though I thought for a moment that I understood, the logic of it all seemed to fall through my fingers like sand.

If only the mountain path could go on for ever like some magical staircase. If only our walk was purely for the purposes of leisure, ending with the two of us returning home refreshed under the pleasant spring sky. We could call out "We're home!" when we arrived home to Mum, who'd be waiting to greet us with a smile, and there'd be no memory of the cancer ever being in her body.

In reality, however, we reached our destination all too soon. We arrived at an abandoned hut owned by a friend and former classmate of Kuma. He mainly kept cows nowadays but as a boy he'd been shown by his grandfather how to slaughter pigs and it was something he secretly did as a favour on the rare occasions when a friend would ask.

Poor old Hermes appeared to be aware of everything – of her destiny, Mum's illness, the troubles between Mum and me, and the indescribable feelings that churned inside me. I crouched down and looked at her, eye to eye, and noticed how her face looked more like that of a wise old grandfather than a grandmother – with her long, white eyelashes, like those of a mountain hermit that sparkled in the midday sun. I stretched out a nervous hand and touched it to her cheek, and in response she seemed to smile for a moment before closing her eyes ever so slowly.

Thank you, Hermes.

We'd spent only a short time together but every moment had been special, and I conveyed these feelings to her in my mind. I wondered if she'd received or understood my farewell message as I walked over to where Kuma and his friend were waiting to grab her gently, but firmly from behind.

"Ringo, are you sure you're ready?" whispered Kuma. "This really is the last chance."

I couldn't say anything and just gave a bow so deep I thought my head might touch the ground. For a moment, I looked at the bugs that were crawling all over my feet. And when I looked back to the sky, the sun was blazing.

Taking a breath, I said a last prayer for Hermes in my mind. Asking that she might pass without pain, that she might leave this world without suffering and that her passing would be quick.

On the count of three, Kuma and his friend flipped Hermes upside down. Then her legs were bound with rope, first the front legs and then the back. They then pushed a pole between her legs and hoisted her off the ground and it was at this point that Hermes began to panic. She started crying out in agony, with a wail like a newborn in the moments after birth, desperately in need of her mother's touch. I closed my eyes but not my ears, and tried my best to take it all in.

I watched the men as they washed Hermes down with water and hung her from the branch of a nearby tree. Though she was unable to move, she was still very much alive. But her wailing had since faded until only the sounds of her breathing reached my ears. Slowly, I approached her, watching her belly inflate with every breath. Then I watched as the men placed a large bucket beneath her, making the preparations sadly complete.

Since I was the leader of today's slaughter, it was my duty to cut the artery. Kuma's friend brought a knife from the barn and handed it to me. Then Kuma pointed to her throat and told me exactly where to cut. I did my best to shut off my thoughts as I raised the knife in the air. Then I brought it down with strength and without hesitation to make it all as painless as possible.

When it was all done, Kuma and his friend seemed quite impressed. They kept saying things like, "What a good pig, eh?" But all I could think of were Hermes's eyes. After a while, the lifeblood that had been coursing through Hermes's body had all drained into the bucket below. We stirred it with a stick to prevent it from congealing so it would be good for making blood sausages later and we were especially careful – trying hard not to waste a single drop of her precious blood.

I treated Hermes's remains with the same gratitude and respect I give to all the ingredients in my kitchen. I've heard this is the way they treat their pigs in Okinawa too. In fact, they say that in Okinawa, they eat every part of the pig except for its cries and I was determined to show the same respect to Hermes.

After the blood was completely drained, Hermes was taken down from the tree and placed on a work table covered with a plastic sheet. We placed her in hot water of about fifty degrees Celsius and used spoons and sharp stones to scrape the hair off her skin. When that was done, we took a burner to her skin to make it smooth.

Then the butchering began.

Kuma and his friend worked together to spread Hermes's legs and fix them in place with a log. Then, once again, they hung her on the same tree branch and secured her in place. Though there are plenty of different types of tools for this sort of thing nowadays, everything that needed to be done was actually possible with just a selection of simple things around us. We took a large axe-like knife to her throat to separate the head from the body. Then we cut a vertical line from the bottom of her stomach to the base of her ribcage. This was actually supposed to be my job as the leader, but because it required a lot of strength, Kuma's friend helped out by standing behind and holding the knife with me. We cut meticulously and carefully, so as not to pierce the intestines. And as soon as a cut was made, some intestines popped out. But since they were still attached inside, they didn't fall out completely. We then put on rubber gloves like the ones doctors wore during surgery and stuck our hands inside, where it was still warm, to pull out her intestines.

We took the plastic sheet that we'd used when scraping off her hair and spread it out underneath her to catch her brightly coloured intestines as they fell. Compared to her large body, her heart looked very small, and when I weighed it afterwards, I found it was only three hundred grams. Now that she'd made the transition from pig to ingredients, each part took on a new name. Her kidneys became the "*mame*", her stomach, the "*mino*", and her small intestine, the "*himo*".

Then came the large intestine and lastly the uterus, which had never been put to any use in Hermes's lifetime but was destined for culinary greatness now. I learnt that animals that give multiple births have two uteri and they were shaped like the bud of a plant that had just popped its head above the soil. Kuma told me they are called "*kob-ukuro*", or "child bags", and wrote the kanji characters for it on the ground with a stick.

Once the intestines were all out, we carried them to a different place and washed them. The next task was to take a chainsaw-like device to split Hermes's body in half and start cutting out the meat. It was heavy work, so I decided to leave it to the men while I went back to washing out the intestines. Several minutes later, Hermes's head was brought over to me, with her eyes still slightly open. Her ears were still soft and her nose still damp and I found it hard to think that this was the same head that had been moving just a short while before. Then I noticed that the corners of her eyes were damp and I began to worry that maybe she had suffered after all.

I'm so sorry, Hermes, I prayed to her departed soul. *But I promise to make you into the most delicious dishes in the world.*

Then, without wasting another moment, I stuck my hand into her mouth and cut out her tongue. One by one, her four legs were carried over to me. And once the bladder was washed clean it was blown up like a balloon and hung from a branch so that I could use it later to make sausages.

By now, the men were busy taking the different cuts of meat – the loin, shoulder, ribs, thighs and chops were all cut up small and put in separate bags before being placed in the shade under a tree. As for the skin, which was mostly gelatin, this was going to be used as the casing for the sausages, so it was also brought over to where I was standing.

Usually, sausages were made by stuffing minced meat seasoned with salt, spices and egg into the intestines. But I'd do that after returning to the eatery. Blood sausage, on the other hand, required the intestines to be very fresh. So I started making them without delay. First, I chopped Hermes's heart and liver and sprinkled salt on them before mixing them with the blood we'd collected in the bucket. I'd decided to use the "full-moon salt", which was a natural salt that can only be gathered by the sea at full moon. Some people said this salt had spiritual powers and I wanted my mum to absorb them.

I chopped the skin into tiny pieces, mixed it in with the fat from the back and some meat from the shoulder and stuffed it all into the washed stomach. All that was left was to let it rest a little and then smoke it to make the blood sausage complete.

Next, I said a final farewell to Hermes's face and placed it in the middle of the work bench. I took a knife and cut off both ears, planning to use them in a salad. Then I cracked the head in two. As my knife went through her head, it let out a sound like a groan. I was surprised to see that her brain was a lot smaller than I'd expected, and with a different, pearl-like colour to it too.

I was going to use half of the face to make a terrine after returning to the eatery and the other half to make a sausage by chopping it up and stuffing it into the bladder. I was relieved to be able to chop the face into pieces without letting a sad thought come to mind, though I handled the meat with the greatest care and respect.

Hermes, as I'd known her, was no more. Never would she cry again, nor snuggle her nose up against me. But in my heart, I wanted to believe that she hadn't really died and that every ounce of her meat contained a part of her dear soul. In this way, I could believe I was somehow wrapped in her warm aura. In this way, I could feel like I was floating in the warm waters of the springtime sea.

I stayed working at Kuma's friend's place right through the evening – through the spring peach sunset the same shade as Hermes's beautiful skin and on until dark. By the time I dragged my tired body back to the eatery, the fridge was already packed with bags of Hermes's pork that Kuma had delivered by cart. There must have been about a hundred kilograms!

During the day, when Kuma and his friend were taking a cigarette break, I heard them saying the quality of the meat was high considering how old Hermes was and that perhaps it was because she was a virgin pig. It was clear even to my eyes that Hermes's meat was of high quality. It was a pretty light pink with just the right amount of fat and it was probably because Mum had always given her top-quality feed.

To me, the meat smelt like a deep forest, with hints of nuts, leaves and soil. The thought of Hermes made me sigh and I decided to boil some water for tea to take my mind off things. I was also ready for a sit down. I'd been standing for so much of the day that my legs had become a little swollen and my shoulders were really stiff – which was unusual for me. As I sipped on the *hoji* chai tea, I thought to myself how I wouldn't be baking bread for Hermes any more even though I still had so much of the natural yeast left. But rather than feeling sad, I was kind of surprised to feel strangely bored. So I picked out a cookbook from the line of books in the corner of the kitchen and flipped through the pages to find dishes for my mum's wedding reception. There was still so much to do for that, so there was no time to waste on being sentimental.

I was trying to put together a kind of trip around the world through my menu. Actually, the original plan had been for Mum and Shuichi to go on honeymoon together. But since Mum had got so weak recently, that was no longer an option. I'm not sure she'd have even had enough energy to withstand the trip to the airport, never mind sit on a plane for an extended period of time. So that's where my idea had come from – if they couldn't travel to taste different foods in foreign lands, then I'd bring those foreign foods to them.

I knew that pigs were raised for their meat around the world and that they were prepared in so many different ways in different countries. So this was as good a place as any to start thinking. I was also looking forward to putting to use all the experience I'd gained through working in so many different kitchens in the past. However, putting together a new menu is no easy task, and from that day on I rarely went home at all. I'd just work through the night on preparing the wedding feast and sleep at the eatery, which I'd temporarily closed.

I began by taking the cuts of meat I planned on using raw, such as the fillet, which I cut the into small, easy-to-cook pieces and wrapped them in cling film for freezing. Then I set about making *char siu* from salted shoulder loin, bacon from the ribs and ham from the thighs. I mixed every odd bit of meat from the head and neck together and used them in salami, meatballs and wieners. For the wiener skin, I was able to get wild sheep intestines from the owner of the farm where the reception was being held.

169

I also tried making prosciutto for the first time. I did this by taking a chunk of loin and covering it with salt and sugar to slowly draw out the moisture. It was Mum's favourite dish and she wanted me to continue to serve it to those who'd cared for her in life, even after she was gone. It would serve as the thank-you gift in return for the condolence money, which was customary for guests to give at funerals.

I knew I had a huge task ahead of me still. There's nothing easy about cooking a whole pig, you know. And in my case, it was both a physical and a mental strain. There was so much I didn't know as well. So whenever I came across something I wasn't sure of, I'd fax the wife of the only butcher in the village for advice. They had a shop inside Yorozuya Supermarket and Kuma had introduced me to them just a little while ago. They were great friends to have, with the butcher's wife being so kind in answering even the most basic of my many questions, which really taught me a lot.

I learnt that the shoulder and shoulder loins were high in fat content, which made them better suited to roasting and steaming. I also learnt that the liver and loin on the thick outer sides of the body were very tender, so it was best to boil them after slicing them thin. The meat around the ribs is full of flavour and the arms are best suited for stews. The thin sliver of fillet you find between the loin and the thigh is soft and lean, which makes it suitable for any dish. In fact, the thigh is so lean that many think it's best to roast it on the bone.

The butcher's wife taught me all this using a diagram that showed every part of the pig. And once I'd got my lessons from her, I began deciding on the actual dishes I wanted to cook. I was also helped along by Kuma and his friends, who kindly donated their free time to help me accrue all the other ingredients I needed.

It was the day before the wedding reception that I finally finished preparing the feast.

I returned home for the first time in quite a while and lay down on my own bed, trying to get some sleep before the early start the next day. The bed in my room was so much more comfortable than the bed of wine crates at the eatery. I realized I must have been absolutely exhausted when I thought back later on and noticed that I hadn't even heard Grandpa Owl's hooting! Then, at just a little past one in the morning, my door slid open and in walked Mum. As I pretended to be asleep, I saw her step over to where I was sleeping and crouch down, peering into my face. I'm not sure why I pretended to be asleep exactly. Perhaps it was out of habit of disliking her for so many years. But as hard as I searched my soul, there was no longer a single bad feeling left for her in my body.

"Ringo," she said, addressing me by my name for the first time in quite a while. And though I wanted to reply, my voice failed me.

"Please, one last time, please say something…" she whispered in a hoarse voice, while gently placing her fingers on my cheek. I kept my eyes closed and pretended to remain asleep, but all the while I concentrated on the feel of her cold fingers caressing my cheek.

Thank you for giving birth to me, I wanted to say. But I couldn't give voice to my thoughts.

I felt so sad, so frustrated and depressed that I almost started crying. I wanted to hug her in apology for everything that had happened in the past but just at that moment, she stood up and quietly left the room. Just for once, I wanted her to hold me. But I didn't have the courage and now I'd missed my chance. My last chance on the night before her wedding day.

Mum and Shuichi's wedding was held in grand fashion on a dairy farm with beautiful greenery. I watched my mother from a distance as she smiled happily atop a white horse owned by Neocon. The wedding dress my mother had spent hours designing before commissioning a tailor to produce was both cute and elegant at the same time. She was wearing minimal make-up, but her skin was still as white as snow. Shuichi was gently supporting her from behind. And pulling the horse was Neocon. Somehow, the sight of the three of them – Mum, Shuichi and Neocon – didn't look all that unnatural. There was even something oddly harmonious about them. Like things were just meant to be this way.

Above all else, the bride was absolutely radiant. I knew this was the beginning of what would be the happiest chapter of her life. And with those thoughts in my mind, I began to apply the finishing touches to my dishes as the breeze caressed my body with the gentle scents of spring.

For me, today's cooking was a prayer. A prayer for Mum and Shuichi's eternal love. A prayer for Hermes who had sacrificed her body. A prayer to the god of cooking who had blessed me with the happiness of being able to cook. It was the happiest day of my life too, and I became overwhelmed with emotion when I saw the large array of dishes sitting atop the tablecloth I'd fashioned by sewing a number of bed sheets together.

Once the bride and groom had said their words of welcome, everyone gathered around the table. There were bottles of champagne everywhere – a generous present from Neocon – and floating in the glass in each guest's hand were cherry-blossom petals that had been soaked in sugar. Kozue was there with her formerly anorexic rabbit that was now her best and furriest friend. It was her mother who'd given us the sugared petals, which she'd made herself from last year's blossoms.

Following a toast, people began digging into the buffet I'd prepared and piling their plates high with my cooking. It made me think of how Hermes was undergoing a kind of transformation, being taken in by the bodies of the guests to give them energy and strength, being given new life through entering another.

All around us, cherry-blossom petals fell from the trees around the farm – trickling through the air and landing on the tables. It was as if the trees were shedding beautiful tears of joy. I bit down on my lip, trying to suppress a smile and some tears of my own. I still had so much work to do. There was no time for tears.

I checked on the wide range of dishes lined up along the buffet table. There was the terrine I'd made with Hermes's head, which I served with pickles made from locally grown vegetables. Hermes's ears were boiled with vegetables and vinegar, then sliced extra thin and served atop a salad drizzled with olive oil and vinegar. The tongue I split in two. One half I used to make a Chinese dish by soaking the meat in a soy-sauce marinade flavoured with five-spice powder and other spices before simmering. The other half I stir-fried with cabbage and seasoned with salt and pepper. The heart went into the blood sausages. The stomach, I salted, and grilled on the spot and squeezed organic lemon over before serving. As for the intestines, I cooked those into a broth made of *hinaizidori* chicken together with Japanese mustard spinach and squid dumplings, before pouring the broth over rice vermicelli and placing a raw egg yolk on it to make a Burmese dish. I took the trotters and stewed them for a long time to bring out the gelatin to make an Okinawan soup. The calves I threw into a pot with a selection of whole root vegetables, which I cooked for several hours to make a pot-au-feu. I chopped the shoulder meat into bite-sized pieces before adding seasoning, coating them in starch powder, frying them in olive oil and tossing them in balsamic vinegar to make an Italian-style sweet-and-sour stir-fry. I also salted and stewed chuck eye roll with watercress to make it into a miso-flavoured soup.

I served the *char siu* I'd made beforehand on its own after carefully slicing it. Then I used some of the slices in a noodle dish with lots of white onions. I stir-fried the chuck I'd kept raw before freezing it with the kimchi I'd pickled this winter. I'd used up most of the rib eye to make uncured ham. Following the butcher's wife's advice, I'd also kept some by the side to slice thinly before boiling it and wrapping it in rice paper with crab meat, bean sprouts and Chinese leeks to make Vietnamese spring rolls. I also used some real *nuoc mam* I'd had specially delivered.

I made the thighs into ham, which I used in sandwiches as well as the potato salad. I defrosted what remained of the thigh I'd kept raw and frozen and roasted it on the bone before serving it with a side of a *yuzu* pepper paste. I minced most of what remained and used it to make a spicy Sichuan *ma po tofu* dish and I made a Turkish green pepper *Dolması* with the little that was left over from that by mixing it with rice cooked in soup and using it to stuff the peppers.

For the rib I'd made into bacon, I mixed cheese into bread dough and baked a bacon cheese bread. I used the natural yeast, which was left behind by Hermes and made chewy champagne bread. The inner side of the spare rib I sautéed with onions and tomatoes before cooking them with cola to make American-style spare ribs. The part with bone I dabbed in wheat before frying it in high-temperature oil to make Chinese-style deep-fried ribs. The fillet, of which there was only a little, I marinated with salt and pepper before frying with small onions and garlic. I added apple and cooked the mixture in a pressure cooker for a few minutes before adding white wine at the end and serving it with sour cream on the side.

Finally, for dessert, I'd made a wedding cake. It was a little clumsy, but it still had a good shape. For decoration, I used a posy of wild dandelions, pansies and roses – all of which were edible. I was especially pleased when Mum, who didn't have much of an appetite, succumbed to eating a slice!

For the tea, Kuma went to the trouble of getting lotus flowers from his relatives in Kyushu. By floating the flowers in the tea, I made the perfect lotus tea with a wonderfully fresh fragrance, which was simply perfect for the reception of Mum and Shuichi.

I also prepared dimple cakes as gifts for the guests. I made a red dimple by taking a brush dipped in red food colouring and lightly touching the tip of a *joyo* cake filled with *ogura* red-bean paste. I'd placed two of them in each box to represent Mum and Shuichi smiling side by side. *If only their smiles could last for years and years*, I prayed as I painted the red dot on each in turn.

Of course, I wouldn't have been able to do all this on my own. It just wouldn't have been possible if it hadn't been for the kind help of practically everyone in the village. In fact I was a little surprised – I'd never realized it, but Mum and Bar Amour had put down some deep roots in this small village surrounded by mountains.

By the day of the wedding, just a glimpse of Mum was enough for people to guess what kind of sickness she was suffering from, and I think that had really brought it home for a lot of the local people, who happily gave their time to help with the reception. And what a reception it was!

Shuichi remained glued to Mum's side, supporting her all the time, and they both wore the biggest smiles I've ever seen on them. All Mum could really manage to do was to be there. She couldn't really eat anything. But she seemed to be keenly observing Hermes's new forms from afar. I think she was happy to know that she was there; that she hadn't gone away. That she'd merely changed form. I was convinced of this as I stared at the empty plates on the table shining under the afternoon spring sun.

I wish I could recall more about that special day. But I'm afraid that if I did, I might crumble. Things like this, the most precious things in the world, I keep them all safely locked away in my chest where nobody can ever touch them. Where the sun can never fade them. Where the wind and rain can never harm them.

And then, just like that, Mum was nothing but bones.

She'd been reunited with the love of her life and made him her husband. I sometimes wonder if perhaps it was the fact that she was able to enjoy married life, albeit for just a few weeks, that had led her to lose her desire to live. Perhaps it was as if her spirit had forgiven her and given her permission to be free. But she remained a happy and beautiful newly-wed to the very end.

Since I had nothing Mum could take with her to heaven, I placed my notebook inside her coffin instead. It was mostly filled with my correspondence with customers, but it also included valuable records of my scarce interaction with Mum. So although I couldn't talk to her, she could still have my words.

Since her passing, I'd been alone in the house with nobody for company but Grandpa Owl. And every night, I remembered the incident that occurred that night before the wedding.

I'd been overcome by feelings of regret that night. Feelings that turned out to be so much heavier than the grief I felt from my mum's passing. My mum had wished so much for me to speak that night, but I'd failed to say a single word. I couldn't stop myself from wondering why I didn't speak, why I'd been such a coward – such a terrible, despicable hypocrite. Somewhere deep down, I knew there was no use regretting things in the past. But it was impossible not to. I knew I'd never see her again. Never speak to her again, no matter if I got my voice back or not. So every night, I dwelt on this until long after Grandpa Owl had given his hoot. And in the days that followed Mum's passing, I kept The Snail closed.

The next day, I went around passing out the prosciutto I'd made from Hermes's roast to all of Mum's friends, acquaintances and volunteers who'd helped out at the wedding. This had been Mum's wish. Kuma went to the houses a little farther out on his small truck, and I went to the closer neighbours on the Snail Mobile. Amazingly, we managed to visit all the houses in one day.

As the seasons kept moving forward, I felt as if my heart had been left behind. The cherry blossoms at the farm had already fallen and the trees were now growing healthy green leaves. But no matter how green and how vital they were, their beauty just passed through the gaping hole in my heart.

One day, I visited Shuichi's apartment. It had been a while since the last time I'd been there. He was my "father" according to the official family registry, but both he and Mum had told me that I could continue to call him simply Shuichi. He'd bought an apartment near the hospital where he worked for Mum and him to spend the rest of their lives in. I think he'd also bought it with her care in mind since the whole place was barrier-free, and there were handrails in the hallways, bathroom and kitchen to make it easier for her to walk around.

Since I'd last seen him, his hair had gone completely white and he'd seemed to age twenty times faster than normal. I couldn't blame him. He'd been through a full and demanding range of emotions – from pleasure and delight to anger and sorrow – all in a period of just a few months. I bowed my head deeply, and handed him the prosciutto I'd made with all my heart. And as we sat down together to have a cup of tea, the conversation turned to my grandmother.

Though I'd had no idea, my grandmother was also a mistress. She was in love with a politician. She'd fallen in love with him when Mum was still young and she'd known he had a wife and kids. But the two had eloped, leaving their families behind, including my mum. That was why my mum grew up without ever being close to my grandmother, because she'd spent her formative years being passed around from relatives to orphanages. I learnt that Mum didn't want her own daughter to go through the same thing. That's why she'd started Bar Amour, so she could work close to home. I wondered if that was why my grandmother had given me so much love, to make up for the love she'd failed to give her own daughter. If only I'd known all this earlier I could have done something to mend our relationship.

That night, tired from meeting so many people, I bathed earlier than usual, and got into bed. I had no foreseeable plans to reopen The Snail and it was possible it might stay closed for ever. After all, with Mum gone from this world, what reason was there for me to stay? Ever since she'd gone, my mind and spirit had been in a daze. And just as I was dozing off with these thoughts going around in my mind, Grandpa Owl started to hoot.

By now, Grandpa Owl was the closest thing I had to family and it made me feel just a little better to be able to hear his call once a day. It was just like when I was a child, when I'd wait to hear his call before being able to fall asleep properly.

"Hoot. Hoot. Hoot." Grandpa Owl kept his rhythm as precise as he always had. But when he finished his ninth hoot, he suddenly stopped. I waited, straining my ears. But the tenth hoot never came. I wondered what on earth had happened. Had something happened in the attic? Could he have been bitten by a snake? This had never, ever happened before. Suddenly, I was overcome with anxiety. The words "alone for life" seemed to come falling from the ceiling to land on the bones in my throat. Shivers went down my spine and I honestly wondered whether my heart might stop.

I'd never peered into the attic before since Mum had always discouraged it. She said that Grandpa Owl was the god of our home, so the attic was his space and we should respect his privacy. But this was different. This was an emergency. And if Grandpa Owl was in danger, then it was my duty to save him. I flung on my nightgown with the floral pattern that Mum always wore over her pyjamas, and I pulled out a flashlight from the emergency bag I kept next to my pillow. Then I climbed into the closet with the flashlight and carefully and gently lifted the panel that led up to the attic.

I couldn't believe my eyes! There was no owl in sight. Not a real one anyway. Instead, there was just an alarm clock in the shape of an owl! I cautiously reached my hand out towards it, feeling the smooth texture of plastic. When I lifted it, it was much lighter than I expected. All these years I'd imagined a real-life owl. So this discovery was so unbelievable to me, it felt like something straight out of a movie! As my eyes adjusted to the darkness, I noticed a letter placed underneath the owl. It had "Dear Rinko" written on it in a familiar hand. It was a letter from my mum.

I came down out of the attic, clutching the letter tightly in my hand. Then I turned on the light switch without wasting even a second, cut open the envelope while taking care not to damage its contents, took out the letter and began to read.

Dear Rinko,

If you are reading this letter, it probably means you figured out the truth about everything. I'm sorry, I never meant to trick you, but that's right, Grandpa Owl is actually just an alarm clock. I'm sure you must have known that in your heart. If it were a real owl it probably wouldn't hoot precisely twelve times every night at midnight, after all. But you're such a lovely, silly girl. I had no idea you'd still believe in Grandpa Owl at your age, but it makes me happy that you did.

It all started when you were young. I felt bad leaving you all alone in the house at such a young age. So for all these years I kept changing the batteries. From heaven, of course, it's not so easy for me to change the batteries any more. So I'm afraid it's time for me to confess everything to you.

How did we become like this? We are like two threads. We can become tangled so easily, but it's not always easy to untangle things, is it? I always adored you, but I was never able to express it to you properly. Maybe somewhere inside me, I couldn't forget that you were not the child given to me by the only man I truly loved. But that's not a good enough excuse, and for that, I am truly, eternally sorry.

Please know that I never, not for a single moment, regretted having you. I couldn't have kept on living like this as long as I did if it weren't for you and Shuichi. Please also know that you are so much cuter and so much more charming than you ever give yourself credit for, my Rinko. You deserve to have more confidence. It doesn't matter if your boyfriend was too stupid to see that. It's time to forget about him. Remember you are my daughter, so it's only natural that you will always have men chasing you!

I also wanted to thank you for the wonderful, precious meal. I'm sure Hermes was very happy, too. She will be waiting for me at the gates of heaven, so even though I'll miss having my lovely daughter and my dear husband by my side, I won't be alone.

I also want you to know that I was so very proud to see you work so hard. It was such a tough time, wasn't it? I know you and your sensitive heart, so I'm imagining you still haven't reopened The Snail, have you? But it's me who passed on, not you! Your life must go on. Plus you still owe me money from the opening and I'm going to want that back some day.

So hurry up and reopen the eatery. There's also something else I want you to do. I want you to save up some money in an old champagne bottle (I think a Cristal bottle would be nice) and bury it somewhere in the farm grounds. Will you do that for me? Then I can go and pick up my savings when I am reborn.

Open The Snail first, though. This is most important. You have talent. You know how to make people happy. And you should keep doing what it is you do best. Spend every minute you can gaining as much experience as possible. And don't hold back. You're cute, smart and an excellent cook. You're someone who is meant to be loved by others. I should know because in my business you have to interact with all kinds of different people, just like you do. So throw your shoulders back, lift your head high and live with pride.

Place your feet firmly on the ground and let yourself breathe. A stubborn child like you needs to go out more, fall in love, and expand your world. The world is so much bigger than you know, and if you set your mind to it you can go anywhere. It's just a flight away, whether you want to go eat hippo meat in Tanzania, or anything!

I guess this is the last message I want to leave for my only daughter. I know we didn't get along so well until the end and that I wasn't like a proper mother to you, but to make up for that, I will be watching over with you with immense power from the other world. I will always be by your side, so you'll always be OK. Remember, a broken heart won't kill you.

And lastly, as for the name, Bar Amour. I bet you thought it was named for the French word "Amour", but it's actually named after the Amur River, which runs through Russia. Shuichi and I had promised each other back in high school that one day we'd go there on our honeymoon. In hindsight we might seem like weird high-school kids for thinking that, but at the time we were dead serious. I must have seen it on a postcard or something, and I'd been completely taken by the river's beauty. I've asked my husband to scatter my ashes in the Amur River. I hope that's OK with you. We weren't able to go on our honeymoon, but I was able to take a trip around the world with your cuisine, so I'm very, very satisfied. I really can't thank you enough and I'm so happy that you are my daughter.

There's also one more thing I need to tell you before I forget. Your umbilical cord is in the freezer in the kitch-en. I know there's nothing you can do with it, but it's unquestionable evidence that you are my daughter. I know you sometimes doubted that, didn't you? One day, when we meet again, I'll tell you the story of how you were born.

There's another thing I have to tell you before I forget. The "Rin" in Rinko doesn't stand for furin! *Seriously, what kind of parent would name their kid "love child"? That was just a way for me to hide my embarrassment. I really named you Rinko with the hope that you won't lead a wayward life like me. I wanted you to live a responsible and hard-working life. To have strong morals and ethics. That's why I took the character from the word* rinri, *meaning "ethics" for your name. It certainly seems to have worked. I'm so very proud of you and I hope you can continue to live your life that way. Anyway, I'm coming to the end of this, my first and final letter to you. When you reach the other side eventually, don't be a stranger. I may have led a wayward life, but please know that in the end I was truly happy.*

With all my love, for ever,

Your mother, Ruriko

Clutching the letter in the palm of my hand, I ran down the stairs into the kitchen and pulled open the fridge door. I found some curry from God knows when, a completely black banana and a half-eaten cake. There was even a crayon lurking amongst the frozen foods and a couple of photos of me when I was young!

In one frost-covered and faded photo, a young version of me was wearing a surprisingly big smile. This was the first time I'd ever realized that there were such happy times in my childhood. For as long as I could remember, I couldn't stand Mum and I clearly remembered my rebellious phase as my tears splashed onto those cold photos.

After taking out all the other objects in the freezer, I came across the box I imagined would contain the umbilical cord, with its surface that had faded to light brown and no words written on it anywhere. I held my breath, and carefully opened the lid and there it was inside, looking like nothing more than a withered old piece of rope.

Mum, I called out silently, wondering if she might be able to feel my words. My mum would always be my mum, no matter what. There were things that would leave to never return and there were things that always remained. There were things that stayed dormant until you sought them out and the world was full of all of these things.

I fell to the cold floor, clutching the cord that had once connected my mum and I, and I felt this might give me the closure I so badly needed. But I couldn't get rid of the deep feeling of regret that clung to me like a bone stuck at the back of my throat.

As early summer came and went, The Snail stayed closed. I spent my days absent-mindedly and without feelings or expressions as I let time simply wash over me. It occurred to me that I hadn't had a proper meal in quite some time. But I didn't want to see blood any more and I really didn't feel like eating. So I chose to eat only the things that had as little life in them as possible, letting my weight drop off and my hair go lank. But I didn't care.

I had instant food for practically every meal and there were days when I had instant noodles for breakfast, lunch and dinner. In fact, I became quite adept at making instant food. So much so that I thought I could change my profession to that of "Instant Food Specialist".

In the pantry there was a pile of instant noodles that were all way past their sell-by date and, since there were no emotions or memories tied to such poor snacks, they were the ideal choice for me. My mum had bought them all and I began to wonder if she got them for the same reason, so she didn't have to think or remember anything painful either.

Whenever I tried to cook anything half-decent, it seemed to only taste of me. It was as if there was no sensation of any food in my mouth at all, leaving me feeling like an octopus chewing on one of its own tentacles or a cat licking its own behind. I learnt then that food is only truly nutritious to the heart and body when someone else makes it for you with love.

A number of hazy days passed in the same way until one sunny afternoon when I was disturbed by a loud crash against the window. I quickly turned around to see a small smudge on the glass and I went outside to investigate. On the ground, I saw a small pigeon lying on its side with blood running down its neck. I leant in to listen to it, but to my great sadness it was no longer breathing. I decided to bury it under the fig tree and gently picked up its little body in both hands. It was the same funeral routine I'd followed every time I came across dead insects, small animals and even flowers. It was also the same thing I'd done with Hermes's eyes and hoofs.

Suddenly, out of nowhere, I heard Mum's voice, as if it was carried on the breeze.

"Death should never be wasted," she said.

There was no question in my mind that the voice belonged to Mum before she got sick and that the message was directed at me. I looked all around, wishing I could see her, so that I could run to her and have her hold me tightly in her arms, just once. But that was the first and last time I ever heard her voice. As the memory of that dear sound faded into the woods, I was left standing there with the dead pigeon in my hands – a pigeon that somehow reminded me of my mum.

I knew the pigeons around here were very clean, feeding only on insects in the forest, unlike the dirty pigeons you see in the city. I also remembered that Kuma had once told me that the wild pigeons around here had a really nice aroma. Suddenly, it all made sense to me! With the pigeon still warm in my hands, I hurried back to the kitchen of the eatery, poured water into one of the pots for the first time in what seemed like for ever and let the pigeon soak awhile.

I carefully plucked the pigeon's feathers. Then I gutted it, placed a selection of herbs in the cavity and sprinkled some salt and pepper on it before setting it aside to rest for a while. I then fried it in a pan with some garlic, and once the surface turned a crispy, golden brown, I transferred it to the oven to complete my first wild-pigeon roast.

I had lost myself in my cooking and lost all track of time, and when I finally came back to my senses, I was surprised to see the sun already setting. The sky was a beautiful shade of orange, looking as if it had been smeared with marmalade and the shadow of the palm tree was growing longer and longer, stretching out along the ground and into the night.

I noticed the sweet fragrance coming from the direction of the oven and thought to myself that the roast should be done in about another ten minutes. So I took out a freshly laundered white tablecloth that was still nice and crisp with starch and spread it out across the dining table.

Then I pulled the cork from a bottle of Amarone, which is an exquisite red wine made with grapes that have been partially dried in the shade, and poured myself a generous glass. For a moment, I enjoyed the light that shone through the glass like rubies, then I closed my eyes and breathed in its luxurious aroma.

As I set out a knife and fork, I couldn't help but think that Mum had borrowed the pigeon's body to come and give me a message. Then I went back to the oven and added a dash of the same red wine to the pigeon juices before plating it up with a liberal amount of gravy.

As I sat down to eat, I closed my eyes and said my blessings, all the while believing in my heart that my mum had come to restore my love of cooking. Then I dug my fork into the wild pigeon that had been soaring through the skies far above only hours earlier. I saw the delicious red juices come flowing out and I cut off a sliver of meat and carried it to my mouth. Immediately, a rich flavour suffused my senses. Then I noticed something strange, but I wasn't sure if I might have imagined it. I took another gulp of wine to calm my nerves and placed another succulent slice of wild pigeon in my mouth. Then, to my amazement, I realized I hadn't been imagining things at all. I knew this was really happening.

"Aaaa."

It was my own voice. My voice had finally come back! I felt as if I'd been carrying a knotted ball of string in my stomach all this time, but now that string had been untangled and pulled from my mouth into the outside world.

"Delicious!" I called out, feeling my throat vibrate and enjoying the thought of my voice leaving my body like a gentle breeze, to fly up to heaven where it could reach my mum's ears.

"Thank you, Mum," I whispered.

In the end, I ate every last morsel of that delicious wild pigeon and all through the meal I felt as if Mum were sitting with me. I'd picked up the carcass with my hands to bite the last juicy pieces from the bones and I'd washed them down with the last of the red wine. I'd saved the pigeon's heart until last, which melted in my mouth and I thought of how both Hermes and the pigeon were now a part of me.

Thinking of Mum's words, I dwelt on the fact that food is something that should never be wasted. And with that, I knew I was ready to cook again; ready for a brand-new beginning, ready to make dinners that make the special people in my life feel happy, ready to cook ingredients that fill people with kindness. They may be simple pleasures, but they are pleasures I can provide for ever. Here at The Snail – the only place of its kind in the whole world.

BORN IN 1973, ITO OGAWA IS A JAPANESE SINGER AND THE author of several children's books. *The Restaurant of Love Regained*, her first novel, is a bestseller in Japan and has been adapted into a successful movie. Ito runs a hugely popular website where she offers daily recipes of Japanese cuisine.